LEGENDS OF THE YORKSHIRE DALES

COLIN SPEAKMAN was born within sight of the Pennines, although not on the Yorkshire side, and was educated at Leeds University. He has worked all his life in the county as a lecturer, officer with the Yorkshire Dales National Park Department, Transport Researcher and West Yorkshire County Council's Tourism Officer.

He is Secretary of the Dales Association, a full-time writer and transport consultant and lives with his wife and two children in Ilkley, Wharfedale, on the edge of the Yorkshire Dales.

North Yorkshire Marketing,
Harrogate, North Yorkshire.

Colin Speakman

LEGENDS

OF THE Yorkshire Dales

illustrated by Julie Garside

ISBN 1 873214 00 6
First published in 1990
(previously published by Allanwood Books under ISBN 0 947963 02 2)

NORTH YORKSHIRE MARKETING
Lambert House, Station Parade, Harrogate, North Yorkshire.

Printed and bound by
Smith, Settle
Ilkley Road, Otley, West Yorkshire.

For Lydia and for Dorian

Never too old to share a well told tale

Introduction

The Yorkshire Dales, one of the most beautiful regions of the British Isles, has its own special literary heritage - a blend of myth, legend, folklore, history and fantasy, its roots lying deep in ancient oral tradition, added to by each successive generation of storytellers.

Now storytelling is one of the oldest and most satisfying of art-forms. Each generation will take the old stories and re-interpret them, re-invent them for their listeners or readers.

But the great stories of the Yorkshire Dales have, for many years, suffered an unjust and total neglect. Some have not been retold for fifty years, some not this century, and some have remained mere footnotes of dusty topography.

So it is high time to take them down from the shelf, blow away the dust of years, and remake them for our age.

And that's what most of these stories are - re-interpretations.

Some have evolved from mere scraps of fact - intriguing fragments of history. I would not dare describe them as history, rather imaginings, flights of fancy, what-might-have-beens, embroidered out of the merest hint - inventions.

Dialogue is an especial problem. To attempt to place it in period would make it unintelligible for a modern reader; with rare exception the characters in these stories speak as they would have done in the 1980s. Dialect, the rich and vivid language of the people of the region belongs, as it should, between friends, family and the familiar. There is no inconsistency, therefore, in the Shepherd Lord switching to polite English when he addresses a courtier.

COLIN SPEAKMAN

February 1986

Contents

The Ballad of Semerwater

It had rained for days. Not the usual kind of rain or drizzle but hard, intermittent downpour with sheets of lashing rain from dark, low clouds that covered the tops above Raydaleside and Cragdale. It was raining before dawn, it rained after dusk and the short, dismal November days seemed like a grey extension of night. Everyone who could sought shelter of house or byre, crouched by fires for warmth.

Out of doors water was everywhere. Becks boiled and roared in cataracts down the hillsides, tumbled in great waterfalls. Meadow bottoms were lakes. The River Bain was a broad, swirling torrent, brown with peat and mud. It was a dark and evil time.

If you were to have looked across the little valley of Raydale which then, as now, forms a sheltered hollow between the high fells, you would have discerned, on that particular afternoon, a tiny figure slowly moving along the ancient track, old in Roman times, which crosses the Stake Pass from Wharfdale to Raydale and Wensleydale. If you'd had enough patience to stand your ground and wait and look again, you'd have seen that it was a figure dressed in black, moving with agonising slowness against the fierceness of wind and rain.

And as the figure drew closer you would have realised it was an old man, bent with age and infirmity, with a great staff in his hand and a black cloak wrapped around his shoulders. At each step he would seem to strike the staff into the ground and haul himself along, limping, his white hair and beard straggled in rat-tails from the rain, his fingers and face red and raw with cold. The clothes he wore were no more than rags, the cloak around his shoulders, once of a heavy woollen cloth, now worn and threadbare with age, tattered around the edges. His shoes scarcely seemed to hold together but squelched as he walked.

Several times he stopped, as if the battering of the wind would force him back and buffet him to the ground. But with a seeming iron-will he would struggle on a few steps before pausing again, thrusting his staff into the ground, dragging himself forward.

Daylight was already beginning to drain away as he reached the edge of the village. He stopped at the first cowbyre, as if he would fall, holding himself upright on the wall corner and seeming to re-gather his remaining strength for a few more hesitant steps.

Ahead was a farmhouse, a comfortable, well-cared-for countryman's home. The old man limped along the path and paused at the door. A light had been lit in the window. Taking his great staff in his hand, he beat three times on the door. There was no response. Again he hammered with his staff.

At last the door opened.

A farmer's wife stood there, a buxom woman with plump arms and cheeks as red as little apples. She looked at the old man with disgust.

'A fine row to make on a respectable person's door!' she said angrily.

'Take pity on a poor traveller,' said the old man in a frail but dignified voice.

'John! John! A vagabond!' There was a noise in the back of the house and husband John appeared with a hayrake in his hand.

'Clear off you old beggar!'

The hayrake was thrust, menacingly, toward the old man's face.

The old man turned round on his heel and without a word made his way down the farmhouse path.

'Clear off!'

The next house, quite nearby, was the village bakery. The baker was already at work, taking a tray of newly-risen dough towards his great oven.

The old man hammered with his staff against the bakehouse door which was hung in two parts. Hearing the noise, the baker put down his tray of bread and flung back the top of the door.

'Take pity on a poor traveller,' said the old man.

As the door opened a waft of warm air, rich with the smell of yeast and crusty bread, met the old man's face. The food and warmth were intoxicating.

'We've enough of thy sort here,' growled the baker, wiping his hands on his white apron. 'Scroungers. Ne'er-do-wells. Give to one, they tell their friends, they all come. Ah'd be out o'business in no time. Tek thissen off.'

The next house was the smithy. The blacksmith was also hard at work by his forge, shaping a horseshoe at his anvil. When he saw the old man's face, made ruddier with the light and heat of the furnace, he roared with laughter.

'Tha's bein int' watter. Do'st tha' want warmin' up?' and he took the half-formed shoe, still glowing, in a pair of tongs and thrust it at the old man so that he recoiled.

'Ah, that's reet,' chortled the blacksmith, slapping his leather apron at his wit. 'We's'l brand thee like a heifer.' And he roared with laughter like a man demented.

Wearily, the old man made his way to the next house, the schoolmaster's, close by the little school. The schoolmaster was making his supper.

'If you need help, old man,' said the schoolmaster, looking sternly over the top of his spectacles, 'then it is surely your own folly. I regret I can do nothing for you. People have to learn the consequences of their own actions. I'm sorry

I can't help you, but I really have nothing to spare. Try the big house.'

At the big house a servant opened the door.

'Take pity on a poor traveller.'

'What is it, Thomas?' said the voice of an elegant lady in a well-cushioned interior. 'Not a tramp? No doubt he's out to rob us. Doubtless there's a dozen of them waiting their opportunity. Get rid of him at once, please.'

Wearily, the old man made his way to each door in the village.

'The Scriptures say nothing about feeding vagrants,' intoned the Parson. 'I know what charity is worth better than to waste it on ragamuffins.'

- and so at each and every door. The rich dismissed him quicker than the poor.

He soon reached the last house in the village. A thin, shabbily dressed man opened the door.

'It's my wife,' he said. 'If it weren't for her, ah'd say tha could come in, but she'll no let me do it; a fearful tempered woman is my wife.'

As the door closed in front of him it was quite dark. Tears filled the old man's eyes and mingled with the rainwater running down his face. The pity of it - the shame.

Yet there was another light ahead in a cottage, on its own, part way up the hillside, up a steep and rocky path.

Could he make it? Drawing on his final reserves of strength, the old man hauled himself up the narrow path, stumbling on rocks, now having to pause for breath, close to exhaustion.

At last, in the complete blackness, he reached the cottage. He could just make out its low roof, thatched with heather. Wearily he raised his staff and let it fall upon the door.

The door opened slowly. An elderly woman, impoverished in appearance, stood there. As soon as she saw the old man her eyes lit with compassion. As he fell forward she held him in her arms.

'Husband - come quickly.'

Between them, the couple carried the old man inside.

It was a poor, mean house, furnished with the plainest wooden chairs and a table. There wasn't even a proper fireplace - the smoke from the fire escaping through the open rafters. Cattle shared the roofspace, their byre and straw bales sharing the human warmth.

Without a word, they took off the old man's sodden clothes, took a blanket from their own bed and draped it around his shoulders. The husband put logs on the fire and hung out his clothes to dry. The wife brought food - oatcake, turnip soup, a little cheese, goat's milk.

'Eat,' said the husband. 'Tha' must be starved.'

The old man ate ravenously, as if he had not eaten for several days. Though the couple had little in their larder, they brought more. The old man ate.

Then they made him a crude and simple bed from straw by the fire. They saw how old, thin and frail he was, his bones protruding through his flesh, his hair silk-fine.

'Stranger, tell us who you are and where you are bound,' said the husband.

But the old man had fallen into a deep sleep.

'He doesn't come from these parts,' said the wife. 'Why dos't tha' suppose he travels this way?'

'Let him sleep,' said the husband.

They covered him with the blanket as if he were a child, tenderly, then left him, to seek their own bed.

But they slept little that night. It was wild and stormy, the gale so fierce that it made the timbers of their little house creak and they huddled together in fear lest the roof above their heads be ripped away by the storm's unyielding fury.

By dawn the wind had died completely away and, to their amazement, they saw bright shafts of sunlight through their window.

They rose to find that the old man was already up and dressed and making preparations to leave. In vain the couple asked the old man to stay longer, to allow himself to recover fully from his ordeal, but he refused.

'I must continue my journey,' said the old man.

They followed him out of doors where, after the days of darkness, the new, bright light dazzled their eyes. The sky was clear and blue. The hillside on which the cottage stood seemed alive with the quicksilver of hundreds of tiny streams, flashing in the light, whilst the becks were cascades of white foam. Colour had returned - the rich browns of moorgrass, bracken, earth. But the river below was fierce, wild, raging.

The old man, his hair now hanging loose and disorderly around his shoulders, stood on a rock overlooking the valley, his staff by his side, like an orator or prophet of old.

Looking down at the valley and the village below he raised his staff and seemed to address the air in a grave and powerful voice:

'Semerwater rise, Semerwater sink
And swallow all the town save this li'le house
Where they gave me meat and drink.'

Scarcely had these words died away when there came, from across the valley, a sound as of distant thunder.

As the man and his wife looked across the valley, they saw a sight they could hardly believe and were to remember for the rest of their days.

The hillside had begun to move. Swollen with water from days of rain, earth had turned to mud, mud to liquid, and the hillside itself began to shudder and shake, the trees sway drunkenly, boulders to roll, gradually at first, but soon gathering momentum as a mighty avalanche carried everything be-

'Looking down at the valley and the village he raised his staff and seemed to address the air...'

fore it - trees, rocks, stones, walls, buildings. Massive boulders were tossed like bobbing corks, great trees splintered. Huge yawning chasms were wrenched open, clay and slurry rolled forward, swallowing everything in its path.

With a shriek of terror the woman realised that the village itself, in the sheltered hollow of the valley, lay in the path of the landslide. The cluster of cottages, farms and church was coming to life to a day it would not see.

There was nothing they could do.

In moments the tidal wave of sludge, mud, rocks and water was upon the village and swept it away like a child's tower of cards. The woman screamed. In seconds all was gone, walls crushed in, roofs shattered, lives ended in suffocating blackness. Water swirled, roared, cascaded, bubbled, took everything before it in a brown and foaming mass. Where there had once been an entire Dales village there now surged the waters of a raw, new lake. Only the little bell-tower of the church protruded above the water and that, too, as foundations crumbled under the surging torrent, slipped away from sight.

Horrorstruck, they turned to the stranger. But he had completely vanished, leaving only the empty fellside above them, the water below.

As the reality of the stricken village came to them, they wept for the pity of it, and finally turned to their tiny home to see what could be made of their lives.

There, in the centre of the wooden table, lay a heap of bright golden coins.

Years, centuries afterwards, when Semerwater had settled to be a place of gentle beauty in its green basin of hills; when trees had grown again and life had returned, even farms, villages, and churches built; when the great scars had healed to be no more than faint hollows in the hillside, then a man or a woman walking by the lake-shore on a still evening in early summer would sometimes pause to hear a bell's faint boom, like a church bell lamenting long departed souls. And so they would listen again, catching their breath to hear the same sound but all they would hear would be the rustling of the wind in the lake-shore reeds.

The Boy of Egremond

Peals of raucous laughter rang across the courtyard.

She looked down from the narrow window of the tower. William had returned, having ridden through the great portcullis on horseback, fresh from the hunt, with a newly killed hart slung over his shoulder.

He was the Golden Boy, the Boy of Egremond, so named from those extensive Cumbrian estates bequeathed to him by his grandfather, William de Meschines, Lord of Copeland.

He had a beauty which would one day become a legend. He was a tall, athletic youth with a shock of flaxen-blonde hair above his handsome features. He had a natural grace and charm beyond his eighteen years and was able to astonish his teachers with the sharpness of his understanding and the penetration of his wit.

She looked down at her son, taking care not to be observed. He dismounted, giving the horse and the prize from the hunt to a waiting servant. Walter Hebeden, his constant companion and son of the Chief Forester, was with him and the two young men exchanged quips and witticisms with the easy abandon of old friendship.

She, Alizia de Romille, in her four and fortieth year, the daughter of an ancient Norman family, took great pride in her family name. It was her grandfather, Robert de Romille, companion of the Conqueror who, after the victories over the Saxons, had been awarded these lands of Craven and who had built this huge castle of Skipton to proclaim his own and King William's authority in this strange, wild land.

Her mother, Cecilia, a lady in her own right, had kept the name of Romille and her many benefactions to the area included the foundation of the Priory at Embsay, close to Skipton. As a girl, Alizia would often be taken there by her noble mother to pray with the Canons.

So when Alizia married into Scottish royal blood, to William FitzDuncan, it had seemed an inevitable and natural thing. FitzDuncan, son of Malcolm, King of Scotland and slayer of the tyrant Macbeth, was long known in Craven for murderous raids on Saxon farms. In more peaceful times an alliance between Scot and Norman overlords through marriage was a balancing of interests.

But within a year the marriage had proved an unhappy one. Though Alizian had been famed for her striking beauty, the novelty of the marriage had soon palled on FitzDuncan. There was a barbarity and a coarseness in the Scot which she loathed whilst he, in his turn, detested her haughty ways and within weeks they were quarrelling openly. He shunned her company and sought refuge in the taverns with hunting companions and with his Scottish cousins. He soon had a reputation in Craven as a violent, headstrong man, vicious in his actions, prepared to beat his servants and vassals unmercifully to get his way.

Yet, in his vanity, he dearly wanted a son to bear his name.

So she acquiesced because she, too, wanted her ancient line to continue. Though their love-making was a brief, cold affair she bore him four children. The first three were all girls, pale, blonde, submissive creatures, their lives circumvented by the rituals of castle and court. Though she was an adequate mother to them - they were largely tended by the household servants - she longed for a boy. A boy who would be powerful, free, able to run with the hunt, shoot a straight arrow, fight like a hero.

And so it came to be. Her fourth child was indeed the longed-for boy-child. She gave him all her love, willed him into strength and manhood. He was a strong, quick infant, soon to walk and talk. He was dressed in the finest silks and linen and, as soon as he could ride, was given a little horse of his own. Even his sisters, who would be expected to burn with jealousy at the favours their brother received, were charmed by his good-natured manner and his generosity to them.

But it is through others that often we live out our dreams.

Alizia, through her son, sought to achieve the power and freedom denied her as a woman. So her son was brought up with men - with foresters, woodsmen, huntsmen, soldiers. They treated him as an equal and were told not to spare him.

By his early teens William de Romille, as his mother insisted he be known, was an exceptional swordsman. He could run like the wind and shoot an arrow as straight and as true as a hawk can fly. He was a fine horseman and understood horses and their ways. The Canons of Embsay taught him to read Latin, introduced him to theology, philosophy, mathematics and he was quick to learn.

She knew he would make an able, just administrator of Romille lands, as well as those inherited from his own maternal grandfather. But he would achieve more. He would become a man of state, a figure at Court, one of the great Barons of England who would help to guide his king and country. His natural warmth of disposition, his wisdom, his sense of compassion to the common people made all who knew him agree that one day The Boy of Egremond would be a noble and just lord.

And so he had grown up and there had developed that close bond betwen mother and son, a bond she had never been able to achieve with her daughters who, as soon as they were of age, were courted by sons of local noblemen and were duly married.

William was her own. And Alizia, alone in her narrow room, would gaze into her little looking-glass and, seeing the deepening lines in her face, the grey strands in her once gloriously beautiful hair, the drying of that once tender white skin, would know that though her own beauty and brilliance had inevitably faded, yet had it returned through the youth and vigour of her son.

She left the room and followed the winding staircase down into the courtyard. Her son had gone, but Walter remained. He watched as the elegantly dressed lady, in her long and intricately embroidered gown and elaborate headress, came towards him.

Both boys had grown up together having been born within a week of each other and, in spite of their difference in station, were like blood-brothers. Yet their temperaments were quite different - William had a bright, open, sunny disposition whilst Walter was more of an introvert, having a sensitivity which, for a lad of his age, was unusual. Alizia knew him almost as well as she knew her own son.

Immediately, she felt something was worrying him.

'Walter - what's the matter? What's troubling you?'

'Nothing, ma'am,' he replied. Then, after a slight pause. 'Well - nothing that makes sense.'

'Tell me about it.'

'I don't really want to. Something or nothing really.'

'I don't believe you,' she persisted. 'Something is worrying you. Trust me. Explain what it is.'

'Well,' he began, hesitantly, 'we were down at the Strid, this morning. We had stalked a deer, though he had thrown us off the scent.'

'Go on.'

'Then I saw it, on the rocks, in the woods, just above the Strid. It was a white stallion, its nostrils flaring, a huge, white beast. It seemed to stand there for a few seconds and then vanish. William seemed not to notice it.'

'I ran up to where I had seen it. But it had completely vanished. Nor were there any traces - hoof marks or tracks. It was just as if it had never been there.'

'Did you tell William?'

'He said I was just imagining it. He wouldn't believe it. But I tell you it was there.'

'How extraordinary.'

'But local people say that a white horse appears at The Strid shortly before someone is drowned.'

A flash of fear went through Alizia's mind.

'Keep away from that dreadful place, I beg you, Walter. Keep William away. For some time. Until the dreadful curse has worn away. Will you promise me that?'

'I will,' said Walter. 'But I'm sure it's only an old wives' tale.'

'Promise me.'

And she turned away to other affairs. But troubled thoughts remained in her mind.

Next day was cool and grey, with a little drizzle in the air. William and Walter had planned a hunt on Cookrise, close to the castle. Their prey was the wild boar, found in the oak and birch woods scattered along the fellside. William was determined to capture a great old boar, leader of the pack, who had eluded them for days. They would hunt on foot, with dogs, armed with short and powerful bow and with sword. It was a dangerous sport, for a boar can attack and inflict a lethal wound.

It was November and the leaves were largely off the trees or turning rich shades of gold and brown where they remained on skeletal branches. It was good hunting weather and the sound of the hunting horns echoed across the still, damp air. Leaves rustled under foot.

Soon the old boar was sighted, heading due east, crossing over the moor. William and Walter were separated from their companions.

At first it seemed as if the beast had outwitted them.

'He's there!' shouted William seeing a dark form dart through the bracken. The beast was weaving through the birch woods. They ran, the dogs barking excitedly behind them. The boar darted to the left, down the hillside, into Wharfedale. They ran on, covering miles.

'This way!' yelled William.

Too late, Walter realised that they were lunging down into the woods above Bolton, towards the Strid. He recalled his promise.

'Come back!'

But it was too late. Intoxicated with the excitement of the chase, William was a hundred yards ahead, his eyes on the prey crashing through the undergrowth like a thing possessed.

The Strid is a beautiful, menacing place; a deep, romantic ravine in the woods where the turbulent River Wharfe is forced through a narrow rocky gorge, a deep fissure scarcely a couple of yards wide where the whole force of the river is concentrated into a narrow, fiercesome torrent, yards deep. Within that torrent hidden whirlpools spin and revolve, sucking down into their depths anything that passes on the surface. All around are rocks pocked and polished by the furious action of the river, whirlpools ground out by spinning pebbles from winter floods, stones carved by the abrasive action of storm-water and sand. In places the fissure is so narrow that a man can easily leap across, especially at the Strid itself, little more than a long stride. There, a tempting but treacherous lip of rock waits to receive the foot. But its angle

'The Strid is a beautiful menacing place - a deep romantic ravine in the woods...'

and height are deceptive and over the centuries many have misjudged the leap and tumbled to almost certain doom in the roaring torrent.

Yet the whole place is hidden in bewitchingly beautiful woods, between steep and jagged crags, a sinister, enchanting place, hauntingly lovely, never more so than in late autumn when the leaves carpet the rocks in gold, brown bracken turns to rust and the luminous green of moss gives a richness, a ripeness, to the scene.

'William - keep away - I beg,' called Walter. But the Boy of Egremond had eyes and ears only for the boar, now resting exhausted on the rocks above the Strid. An arrow clattered onto the rock a yard short. William reloaded but the boar, suddenly alert to the danger, rose to its feet. Cornered, it hesitated for a moment as if deciding whether to attack its approaching assailant then, thinking better of it, summoned its final reserves of energy to thrust itself across the terrifying mouth of the Strid. It landed heavily on the other side and appeared to slip, its trotters desperately seeking purchase on the muddy embankment before rushing heavily into the wood.

'William! Stop!' Walter shouted desperately.

But William only saw the prey was his. The boar was exhausted. He would slay it on the other side.

He slipped the leash around his hound and stepped towards the Strid, a leap he had made many times.

But his dog, terrified of the roaring water, now swollen by autumn rains, suddenly held back. The Boy of Egremond's wrist was jerked as he leapt. His foot, though perfectly judged, slipped a little on the wet rock and the sudden pull on his wrist from the dog's leash caused the disaster. He plunged headlong into the foaming torrent, pulling the dog after him.

The force of the water sucked him under, forced him underneath the deep, hollow, rocky shelves which lie under the lip of the Strid, trapping him by weight of water so that after a few terrifying, choking seconds he knew only oblivion.

Walter, white with terror, flung himself to the lip of the rock but there was nothing to be seen but swirling bubbles.

He ran up and down the embankment for several seconds, calling frantically...

'William, William, William!!'

No sign of his friend. He ran desperately up and down, flinging himself to the edge of the water, looking downstream. Suddenly there was a flurry in the water. He rushed down, joyous. It was the dog, half drowned but because of its lighter weight, flung free. The creature scrambled on the bank, whimpering with fear.

Of the Boy of Egremond there was no sign.

Then Walter became aware of a white shape in the water, where the Strid finally plays itself out and becomes a broad river. He plunged into the water.

It was indeed William, lying face downwards. With the strength of desperation Walter tugged and dragged his friend to the bank.

But it was all over. The lungs, filled with water, were those of a drowned man. The eyes were open and upstaring. Frantic, Walter rubbed the hands and face. But the blood was stilled in the veins. A few minutes ago there had been life and vigour; now there was only this dead thing. He had gone forever.

'William!' It was a cry of pain.

Through the confusion of his thoughts, Walter knew he must seek help. He ran back up through the woods to a woodman's cottage where two men were chopping logs. They ran back with him to the lifeless form lying on the riverbank.

Simple, powerfully-built men they, too, saw that nothing could now be done for the young lord. So they improvised a simple stretcher of branches and twine and placed the Boy of Egremond on it and carried him up to the road.

By now, other members of the party had joined them and they formed a melancholy procession, following the felltrack over to Embsay and Skipton, taking turns to carry the bier.

They approached Skipton town as night-fall came upon them. As they came in sight of the castle, Walter's heart was filled with an even greater dread. This was something he could not evade. He ran on ahead, into the castle, thrusting himself up the stairs of the tower, into her room.

At first she was startled by his unannounced visit. Then she saw the muddy, dishevelled appearance and at a glance knew all.

'What good is useless prayer?' he asked.

She gazed at him, her eyes filling with tears.

'Endless sorrow,' she replied, and they wept in each other's arms.

* * * * *

For months, Alizia de Romille, heartbroken, seldom left her room. The funeral had been simple and dignified, attended by her estranged husband who, for a time, had been shattered by the grief but sought no reconciliation, and by her daughters the eldest of which, Cecily, would now inherit. But Alizia was inconsolable. For her, everything she had cared for was at an end.

One morning at the end of that winter, a visitor begged to see her. It was Father John, Prior of Embsay. He was an elderly man in his sixties with snow-white hair and kindliness in his eyes.

'My lady, I beseech you. We come to share your suffering and sorrow. The love of God is with you.'

He held out his hand to her, a pale, scholar's hand. She looked at him in his thick, black habit, the austerity of his dress contrasting with even her own costume of mourning. Something in his manner touched her deeply.

'Father, my son and I gave you land by the River Wharfe - the treacherous Verbeia of the Romans - who took his life. Bring your Priory there; let it rise in a place of beauty and of learning, a symbol of what he was and what he might have been. I will give that which you need to do it.'

For answer the old man went on his knees and kissed her hands.

'And others, in time to come, and in ways we cannot yet imagine, will come to that place and rejoice.'

Some weeks afterwards, as the late Dales spring finally let the oakwoods of Wharfedale break into leaf, Walter de Hebeden joined the little band of Black Canons and lay-brothers digging out foundations, laying roughly cut stone from the nearby quarry, on a headland by the River Wharfe near Bolton village. A curlew flew overhead, disturbed at the tapping of the mason's hammer.

Walter stood up from his work. The fresh light of May glistened over the river as it flowed gently, expansively, around the bend of the headland, the brown water contrasting against the new greens of the woods. Beyond, the noble outline of the fells offered a timeless beauty.

In spite of himself, Walter felt a warm feeling of emotion, something which eased the pain in his heart which, for six months, had been a burden to him. At that moment he knew that he would soon take vows and pledge himself to the little community settling by the Wharfe. But what he could scarcely have guessed was that within three decades he, Walter Hebeden, would be elected by his brethren as the third Prior of Bolton Priory, long respected for his wisdom and learning.

Nine Standards

Scots!

The word a scream of terror. The word a wall of flame, searing flesh. The word an axe lunging towards the unprotected skull.

There was no warning. They took the little hamlet at dawn. No time to seek protection behind the stone walls of Pendragon, or Lammerside, or even within Kirkby Stephen kirk. No time to grab a protective shield or pike. No time to flee.

It was a band of no more than a score of wild, ragged men, cattle thieves, butchers, rapists, murderers. No doubt a foraging band from the main army, spying out the land, seeing what rich picking could be found.

Alan had been up early, attending to a sick calf. Suddenly there were shouts, screams. For reasons he could never later fully explain, or justify to himself, he didn't leave the byre, but leapt up the ladder into the hay-loft. He could hear the splintering of wood as they smashed a door down, screams, harsh gutteral shouts in a tongue he didn't understand.

What should he do? He hesitated, trembling. He looked round for a weapon but there was only the scattered remnants of last summer's hay. Not even a broom. Without a weapon he would be cut down like a thistle in a field.

Suddenly they were there, below him. He held his breath. They saw the cattle and led them hurriedly outside, their booty. Others of them were attacking other houses. There were screams, shouts.

He crouched, out of sight, transfixed.

Maybe they should have known that one day this would happen. The raids had come further south each year, ever since Bannockburn. They had heard what had happened further north, further east but they never imagined it would happen in their quiet valley. It was so small a settlement, barely a half dozen cottages and farms under the great crag of Mallerstang Edge and now they had been discovered.

Why?

Tears of anger and frustration. If he rushed out he would be killed.

But now there was something else. The acrid smell of smoke. They were firing buildings. Not only had they seized everything else of value, the means of livelihood and life, but were destroying life itself and leaving utter destruction. It was wanton, vicious, cruel, pointless. Alan knew he was staring into the face of evil itself and it terrified him as much as the holocaust outside.

Smoke was suddenly everywhere. Flaming brands were thrust onto the thatched roofs, catching the dried heather and ling. The wooden buildings quickly caught fire.

In what seemed to be moments the air was thick with dense, choking smoke and he tried hard to contain his tell-tale coughing. Then the flames were suddenly there, vivid yellow walls of fire. He would be smoked out like a rat and slaughtered. The flames were closer, the heat began to blast towards him.

Desperate, he leapt down from the hayloft, flung himself through the wall of flames into the farmyard. Chaos was all around - thick smoke, chickens, shadowy figures. He was leaping a wall, running for precious life, across the small outfield behind the farm, up the fellside. He ran towards a little gill, instinctively flung himself into the shallow ravine and concealed himself, his heart and lungs bursting, his eyes running with tears caused by the smoke.

He must have lain there some hours conscious that if he was seen he would be hunted down. But when, finally, he summoned nerve to rise up and look down towards the hamlet, a scene of total devastation greeted his eyes. Every farm and dwelling-house, every barn, had been destroyed. A thin pall of smoke hung over the valley. He looked across at the vast, flat-topped shape of Wild Boar Fell that formed the other side of Mallerstangdale.

The plunderers had gone, apparently back the way they had come, along the Eden, no doubt, with booty enough to keep them content for one more day.

But why this total, senseless destruction?

He looked at the blackened shells with a sense of horror and foreboding. There was no sign of life there. He made his way down the fellside.

Their farm was merely a line of blackened stakes. The roof had burnt away, fallen in. Trembling he looked through the still smouldering remains inside the house. In the corner of what had been their main room lay what appeared to be two charred bundles of rags.

He turned away, sickened with horror. There was no need to see more. Desperate to escape that evil place where he, too, should have perished, he walked a few yards, then stopped, plunged into the misery of grief and despair.

How long he stayed there, crouched with his head in his hands, desperately trying to wipe out from his mind that which he had seen, he could not tell. He was aware of movement, someone near him. Alarmed he looked up.

It was a child.

She was no more than eight or nine years old and, bewildered, her face lined with dirt and tears.

He held out his hand to her. She took it, silently. Without saying a word he rose to his feet and turned with her to the road which lay away from the hamlet. They both instinctively knew that they had to get away from that dreadful place. She was a neighbour's child, he knew her well. She too had been orphaned by the marauders. He would protect her. Coward that he had been, he had been spared to save this child.

So he walked with her up the long road which climbs the shoulder of the valley, forming the ancient Highway into Wensleydale, a road as old as civilisation itself.

After some little time, at the head of the pass, they came to a steep rocky ravine, a deep gorge where the stream that forms the river Eden comes tumbling down in white foam across the rocks. They crossed a slender, rickety wooden bridge. He held her hand to steady her. It was a wild, desolate place known as Hell Gill.

Alan wanted to press on, in case the raiders returned. In another hundred yards or so, another stream crossed the path. This was the beck that formed the River Ure of Wensleydale. They stopped for a few moments, to drink its chill, pure waters and wash from their faces the sweat, acrid soot and tear stains.

So far they had not uttered a single word to each other.

'Art tha' hungry?' he asked her.

For answer she nodded her head. She was a slim child, her ragged dress torn and stained. One day perhaps she would be able to tell him how she had escaped. They had shared so much, for them a major tragedy which would not be even a footnote in recorded history. She could have been his sister; he was himself barely nineteen and on the threshold of manhood.

'Look!'

She pointed along the path, the way they had come. A man was running towards them. Instinctively Alan pressed the child protectively towards him. But it wasn't a raider. As he came closer it became clear that this was a man dressed in the heavy habit of a monk. He had been running hard. He was, as far as Alan could judge, a man in his late thirties or early forties, of taller than average height, lean, bronzed as if used to an outdoor life.

'You come from Outhgill?'

Alan nodded.

'Then God in His mercy be praised that you have been spared.' The monk made the sign of the cross.

At that point Alan felt that there was little to thank God for, but it seemed inappropriate to make any such observation.

'My name is Brother Matthew, from Jervaulx. I came upon remains of the village and assumed all had perished. The devastation around Eden and Mallerstang has been total. Then I saw you ahead and guessed you had come from the village.'

'I am Alan, son of Robert of Outhgill,' said Alan. 'This girl is Catherine of Hartleys. Our parents died in the raid. We travel to safety.'

'Then travel with me,' said Brother Matthew.

The monk explained that his Abbey owned farms in Cotterdale, in the next valley, where they would be given shelter.

They continued through the grey afternoon, the heads of the fells capped in a low mist although it remained mild. Soon they reached the farm at High Dyke, then followed the fellpath into the lonely wastes of Cotterdale.

They came down the hillside to reach a small farm, a grange of the Abbey where lay brothers managed a network of small farms and sheep-walks.

'In days gone by,' explained Brother Matthew, 'the Monastery was founded at Fossdale, the next little valley to this. It was here that the early brethren began to clear the land, before moving down to a kinder place near Askrigg town, then to Jervaulx where we are now, beyond Middleham.'

They were welcomed in the grange, given hot soup, cheese, oatbread. After supper, they sat by the great open hearth whilst Brother Matthew spoke of his fears for the Yorkshire Dales.

'Since King Edward's army was defeated at Bannockburn by the Bruce,' he said 'each year they have come further - burning, pillaging, looting. Nothing is sacred - not man nor beast. They take and plunder at will, kill and ravage. They know the King is a weak man; they come without fear of reprisal. For us Bannockburn was a black and terrible day.'

He stopped, staring into the fire. Alan could see the intensity in those dark eyes. This was not a man to be trifled with.

'Already Bolton Priory in Wharfedale has been plundered. They have come as far south as Pontefract and Airedale in the east, and Wharfedale in the west. They are finding their way into the side valleys, hitherto ignored. No man or woman is safe from the scourge.

'Last year we tried to fight them. I was with the great Archbishop Melton whose army of monks and churchmen met the invaders at Myton on the Swale. But we were no match for them. Our weapons were simple, our men untrained, and though we believed we had God on our side, it was insufficient. We were cruelly defeated and the Scots swept westwards into the Dales, capturing Bolton Priory and even raised Skipton to the ground. I only just escaped with my life.'

'Each year they grow more audacious. Our king does nothing to defend us. Many of the barons, instead of defending their homeland, do treacherous deals with the foe to ensure the safety of their own carcasses whilst their countrymen are, like your own father and mother, put to the sword.'

'I will fight to avenge them,' said Alan.

'Indeed you will, my son,' continued Brother Matthew. 'But we must first understand the treachery within our midst. How was it that the foe that burned your home did not touch Pendragon Castle, seat of the wretched Andrew Harela? If only our king would come and defend his realm.'

Angrily he slapped his fist onto the palm of his other hand.

'It is as if our London king neither knows nor cares what happens to the Northland,' said Brother Matthew. 'We must perish or prosper by our own efforts alone. So many people say this new curse is 'the will of God' as if it were a plague or the weather. But I tell you this, Alan, what you and I saw today is not God's Will. God alone can help us prevent it, but we must fight to achieve His Will.'

'To my last drop of blood!' said Alan. The hateful images of the charred corpses and ruined house kept returning like an evil dream before his eyes.

'May God be with you,' said Brother Matthew, taking the youth's hand in his.

Catherine, exhausted from her ordeal, lulled by the warmth of the fire, had fallen asleep. They lifted her up and carried her to a little makeshift bed in the corner of the room.

Next morning, Brother Matthew left early for his parent abbey at Jervaulx, there to relate to the abbot all that had passed. Alan and Catherine were to remain at the Grange at least until it was considered safe to return to Mallerstang. But who was left to rebuild the farm or to bury the dead?

Life at the grange was harsh but far from intolerable. Alan was treated as a lay-brother, given specific tasks, hoeing land, tending sheep, rebuilding walls. It was a life he knew well and he quickly set to work with a will, soon earning a reputation for hard work and honesty.

Little Catherine was fostered on one of the grange farms in Cotterdale. A kindly middle-aged man and his wife took care of her, gave her tasks to perform to suit her age and aptitude. It was a hard, yet satisfying life in the upper Dale. Thin soils and a cold, bleak climate made it difficult, even in an average summer, to ripen anything but the toughest corn and oats, far more tolerant of harsh conditions, were the staple fare.

Yet for Alan, forgiving and forgetting were impossible. The flames, the screams, came again through his nights like a recurring nightmare. He knew only vengeance would help to exorcise his sense of grief and despair.

As the days of summer shortened to autumn, the nights getting colder and longer, he would often reflect. What would happen if they came again? He would rather die fighting than live with the shame of defeat and despair.

Brother Matthew visited them quite often. His role was to travel between outlying granges to establish important trade and produce arrangements for the monastery. Alan soon learned that he was highly regarded by the abbot for his energy and his organising skills.

So it did not come as a complete surprise to be asked, one late autumn morning, to accompany Brother Matthew to Jervaulx itself.

It was a full day's journey along the length of Wensleydale to the Abbey. Until now, Alan had never travelled more than ten miles from his home and he was amazed to see the rich beauty of the landscape, the wooded hillsides, famous for their deer, the great sheep-walks, the little stone-walled enclosures around the farms and villages. They made their way through the great hunting forest of Wensleydale which lay between Bainbridge and Middleham, the rich woodlands, where even the grazing of sheep was rigorously controlled to allow the woodland to regenerate naturally. He enjoyed seeing Askrigg, already a busy little township with four or five workshops.

They forded the river near Redmire and made their way along the winding road through West Witton and up onto Middleham Moor. Looking back across the river they could see the massive bulk of Bolton Castle. But ahead was Middleham Castle with its own grand towers.

'A fine defence against the Scots,' observed Alan as they walked through the town's cobbled streets past the thick battlemented walls of the castle.

'But no defence for the common people,' said Brother Matthew. 'Skipton has a great castle, but it did the townspeople no good when the Scottish army came.'

It was already growing dark as they approached Jervaulx Abbey. Alan had never seen such a fine building, nor such a community of people, all following the carefully organised tasks they had been allotted. They ate a good meal, with meat and a pot of small beer, in the great refectory, and retired to bed early. Alan was given a simple but comfortable straw mattress in the lay-brothers' dormitory.

He was wakened before dawn next day and went with the other occupants of the dormitory to attend early morning prayers, all carried out in a tongue which he knew was Latin but could not comprehend.

Soon after a simple breakfast of black bread and beer, he was directed into a large room, its narrow windows giving it the appearance of a church. Almost everyone, apart from himself and two or three other young men, were monks or dressed in monks' habit.

They rose to their feet as an elderly man appeared.

'The abbot,' whispered his neighbour. He was a frail and venerable man and bade the gathering sit on the stone floor.

'Brethren,' began the Abbot, 'we are here today to speak of the terrible affliction amongst us. Such is the Will of God. I believe we can only meet this terror by the force of prayer and anything else will be in vain. But I will hear you speak in turn.

'Brother Matthew, it was you who urged us to come together to talk of what could be done in the name of the Almighty. I beg you to speak.'

Brother Matthew rose to his feet. Within moments Alan realised he was an eloquent speaker.

'My Lord Abbot,' he began, 'I have with me today a young man, Alan Robertson, who only a few months ago witnessed the unholy murder of both his parents before his very eyes, who saw his home and his livelihood destroyed by vicious and ignorant men. I want you to reflect that this happened because these bestial creatures knew that they would escape retribution.'

'I ask you, Lord Abbot, if you truly believe that it is the Will of God for good, innocent people to suffer in this way? Is it the Will of He who created the world that His children should suffer torment and death? Would He not support and help those who fought to destroy his enemies?'

'So, Brother Matthew, what would you have us do?' asked the Abbot, sensing a groundswell of support for Brother Matthew's fighting words.

The monk outlined his ideas. Each year, as the snows melted, as predictable as the early swallows, the raiders would come.

But this year there would be a surprise for them from the Dalesmen of Yorkshire. This year it would not be a question of such easy prey.

And so a group of monks and lay-brethren, including Alan, were set to organise the preparation of defences. This involved making simple but effective weapons. The abbey had a small iron-furnace and simple weapons were cast, spiked pike-heads to put on poles, even a kind of crude sword which, though it was not of fine steel, would suffice. Shields were made of oak, studded with iron nails. Simple armour was fashioned, crude breastplates and helmets completed the arms.

'It doesn't matter if they're not too strong,' explained Brother Matthew. 'As long as they look good. True defense is a matter of deceiving the other side, making them think they're a lot weaker than you are.'

And so they worked with a will, making a variety of ferocious looking weapons, dyeing plain rough-spun cloth to look (from a distance) like chain-mail.

But strangest of all, Alan was deputed to travel, with a small group of men, over to Birkdale, at the very top end of Swaledale. There, at the highest point of a broad-topped fell overlooking the Birkdale pass between Swaledale and the Eden Valley, they had been instructed by Brother Matthew to build nine tall cairns of stone, twice the height of a man.

They had to work through the bitterly cold weather of late winter, with

'...they had been instructed by Brother Mathew to build nine tall cairns of stone, twice the height of a man.'

snow on the ground and freezing wind blowing across the fells. To keep out the cold, they improvised simple sheepskin coats, with the warm fleece inside, and caps of rough 'bump' wool. Simple pigskin mittens protected their hands from the burning cold.

'Yon's lost 'is wits,' said a young tenant farmer, referring to Brother Matthew, as he and Alan worked alongside each other, breaking flat stones away from an improvised quarry face to carry up to the summit.

'If tha's a mind ter stay alive and luck after thi' land, tha's best 'old thi noise and get mair steeans' responded Alan.

'But what's it fer? This'll nivver knock down Scotsmen.'

'Tha'll just see.'

So the great, tall cairns gradually rose on the hilltop. Alan had to admit that they were a grand sight and, if the day was clear, it was a magnificent view from the top of the fell down into the Eden Valley.

But there wasn't much time. Already the days of April were turning milder, the snows were melting in the valley. Brother Matthew himself came to view the work.

'Excellent,' he said, observing how carefully the stones tapered to make a strong, firm tower.

'Appen there's good Dales wallers mekkin' them,' said a voice behind him.

Brother Matthew insisted a long pole be inserted in each cairn and for the allotted day a large colourful flag be prepared ready to rise on every pole.

'ees lost 'is wits,' said the farmer. 'I told thee.'

A small band of volunteers were gathered, no more than twenty strong, Alan among them. They were to be given the uniforms, taught how to handle the arms. They were to stay for a few days in Kirkby Stephen. Strong runners were organised, look-outs placed in strategic points. Men were briefed.

Brother Matthew, himself, took charge of the operation. The Dalesmen obeyed his every instruction to the letter. Had he been a trained military man, the discipline and sense of purpose he gave them could not have bettered.

* * * * *

Almost a year to the very day that Outhgill had been destroyed they came, the Scots. Brother Matthew had the whole strategy planned to perfection.

As soon as the look-out came with the words 'The Scots', the little Dales force took up their position, concealed behind a small hillock above the main highway into Mallerstang.

The Scots were a wild and ragged mob, perhaps two or three hundred strong, dressed in kilts, with long, unkempt hair, armed with axes, pikes, short swords. They had come down from the Borders, living off the land through which they passed but, in an area already blighted by their pillaging and burning, they had determined to come further south into the rich pastures of Richmond and of Craven to enjoy new prey. Alan recognised, with a feeling of utter dread, the strange gutteral tongue he had heard when his parents had been murdered.

Suddenly Brother Matthew, dressed as a warrior, sprang into their path. The others surged behind him. They were a tiny band barely twenty strong and hopelessly outnumbered, but the Scotsmen would have to cut them down to continue their way.

'Where is he among you that speaks the English tongue!' roared Brother Matthew, holding his sword before him. He was an impressive sight. Yet Alan could see that he was trembling, perhaps with fear.

'Ach Sassenach, out of the way before we slice yer doon,' came a voice.

'Hold. I come here to offer you your lives.'

'Ach, and what de ye think yer mean by that?'

For answer, Brother Matthew waved his sword toward the fell. As if in answer, flags began to unfurl on each of the nine great cairns on the summit ridge.

'Each of those banners' declared Brother Matthew, 'stands at the head of a thousand men. An army of nine thousand men from the whole of Yorkshire awaits you. Every dale has sent its sons, every valley its finest warriors, to defend their kingdom.'

'You lie,' said the spokesman, a tall red-haired Highlander who, by now, had pushed his way forward, sword and round shield in hand.

'See for yourself,' said Brother Matthew, looking the Highlander directly in the eye. His opponent looked up at the fell.

'Then why d'ye no tek us by ambush?'

'Because we are Christians and do not wish to see unshriven souls thrust with their sins upon them into Perdition.'

'For I tell you,' and he looked across at the ragged throng. 'our kindred-folk seek bloody vengeance for that which they have suffered. Not one of you will live to see the close of this day. There will be weeping and mourning in the Scottish Glens tonight.'

'But today is the day of Saint Helen, great patron saint of our Yorkshire Dales and I am sent, in the name of King Edward to offer you opportunity to make a safe withdrawal. Otherwise each and every one will perish by the sword.'

There was a pause. Then shouts. A rock hurtled forward.

'Kill them!' shouted another voice.

It was a tense moment. It seemed to the little band that the great body of Scots was about to surge forward, to overwhelm them. But the Dalesmen stood there, looking like a well-armed and well-disciplined force.

The big Highlander turned to his troops and for a few moments addressed them in Gaelic. There were murmurings, but the Highlander gestured towards the hill, towards the Nine Standards. By the cairns, small figures could be seen moving, as if by a great encampment.

There was discussion, hesitation, gestures. Finally, the big Highlander turned back to Brother Matthew.

'Sassenach, hear this. What you have shown us here today has persuaded us to yield, for we are so outnumbered. But I swear we shall return.'

'And, Scotsman, I swear we shall greet you with a handshake of iron. But today go in peace and in pride because no blood shall be spilt.'

And Brother Matthew held out the hand of truce, of peace. The Highlander took it.

The Englishmen watched as the Scots turned, their leaders first, back through the silent crowd along the road to Stainmoor. Many seemed confused, unsure if they had sustained defeat or victory. Nor could the Dalesmen be sure that treachery would not occur.

They waited, tense until the long, ragged army began to disperse. The tail-enders were little more than lads, boys, children, thin and hungry, with what appeared to be makeshift swords. In spite of himself, Alan began to feel pity for them, a realisation that they were starving. It was about hunger, this march. But why the senseless killing?

As the straggling tail of the invaders vanished out of sight a great burst of uncontrolled laughter broke from Brother Matthew, laughter of relief.

'It worked!'

They found themselves laughing, singing, then joining the monk by the roadside in a prayer of thanksgiving.

'Is it really St. Helen's Day?' asked Alan later.

'Perhaps. I really haven't the faintest idea,' confessed Brother Matthew. He had insisted the little party returned towards Wensleydale through Mallerstang and the old Highway.

Alan dreaded passing his old home, where his parents had been murdered. But when they arrived at Outhgill, there was a pleasant surprise. The farms and cottages were being rebuilt. Charred timbers and rubbish had been cleared away.

'I would like you to return. There is work to be done. But first, something for you to see.'

There, by the beck, on a small patch of land were simple mounds and stones on the raw, new earth.

'It was impossible to find consecrated ground. So they are buried here. I have had words with the bishop. The ground is to be consecrated. One day, perhaps, a small chapel will be erected here...'

'And little Catherine. You must arrange for her to be brought here. We must see what we can do for her future.'

Alan looked at his friend and mentor, still dressed in his imitation soldier's uniform. It was such men of indeterminate background, of vigour and courage, who helped to change the course of history. Yet he would now blend into the background, the eternal diplomat, civil servant, arranger, creator.

Alan looked across the valley. Wild Boar Fell, massive, imposing, majestic, a sight he had known from birth. Yes, in spite of all the dangers, all the uncertainties, it was worth fighting for.

He would return.

The Race

For Adam, it was one of those moments of indescribable horror which forever blemish a life. He recalled every detail with an agonising clarity. One moment riding through the Forest on an unfamiliar track, looking for poachers, the next flung headlong as his horse stumbled and fell into a deep pit, the massive weight of the beast crashing on top of him.

It was a deer-pit, built, without doubt, by poachers to catch the King's deer. It was a pit covered with light branches and bracken intended to collapse under the weight of a stag or wild boar, to which the poacher could return at dead of night and under pain of death. It was a common enough hazard for a young Forester in a Royal Forest, but it was Adam Haveragh's undoing.

After such a fall, he was lucky to be alive. His crushed body lay bleeding for some hours before he slowly regained consciousness. The horse was dead, its neck broken. As he came to his senses, he dragged himself from under the horse but was aware of a strange numbness in his legs. They wouldn't move.

Painfully slowly, each movement of his body causing him spasms of pain, he managed to haul himself up by clutching at tree roots and stones to reach the edge of the pit, always anxious that he'd slide back on the wet mud. As he crawled out it was growing dark, so he pulled himself on his belly to the edge of the main track and, rolling himself in a makeshift bed of bracken, slept till dawn.

And so they found him, early next morning, more dead than alive. They carried him to his mother's cottage and she wept to see the state he was in. She stripped off his torn clothes and washed him as she would a child, and bathed his wounds. For days he lay in a fever, hovering between life and death, but slowly, gradually, the old life, the spirit came back into his eyes and she knew he would live and thanked God for it.

But when she saw that he would never walk again but always remain a cripple, she wept once more. Something within his body had snapped that fateful day. The muscles in his legs were useless and the limbs simply would not function but hung, wretchedly. Rough crutches were made for him by a kindly neighbour and he soon learned to use them and could hop along with great energy and vigour, swinging himself around with dexterity. But people were not deceived.

'Such a fine young man he was too,' clucked the neighbours. 'And she a widow-woman'. For they knew, as his mother knew, that all was spoiled.

What use is a cripple? A cripple couldn't be a King's Forester; a cripple couldn't farm, or hunt, or wed. A cripple couldn't mend fences, dig ditches, clip a sheep. Unless he learned a craft with his hands, spinning or weaving perhaps, then he couldn't earn his bread. And what would happen when his mother was too old to tend her cow, pigs, hens and square of land? Why, there wasn't even a living for the old woman, let alone for her crippled son of one-and-twenty.

So Widow Haveragh thought long and hard about what she might do for her poor son. At least his life had been spared. But how would they live?

She began to think to herself through the long winter evenings. She realised too that, though he was cheerful in his manner, underneath lay a deep sadness. Though he would do what jobs he could for her, laying down his crutches to chop wood or milk the cow, she would often find him staring into the Forest, preoccupied. She knew what he was thinking.

If only they had some more land - a few extra acres. They could keep a few more cows, pay someone to help them; there'd be enough for a better living. In the past people had actually been allowed to take in a bit of the ancient Knaresborough Forest, at the edge of which was their own cottage. But King Edward would not permit it and anyone attempting to build on the reserve was ejected brutally by the King's Foresters. Was there land to be found down the Washburn, where the deep valley swept down to the fast flowing stream? But all the land was owned by wealthy barons, powerful, greedy men. And they had no money to buy even the meanest strip.

What about Prince John, Duke of Lancaster? He now owned that great estate from which her husband's family had originally come, Haveragh Park, a great walled enclosure or parkland used for the breeding of the king's horses and for royal deer. The king had recently given that Park to the prince who had the reputation for being a kind, generous and just man.

'Maybe we must go and ask him,' said the widow. So it was agreed that when the prince next came to Knaresborough, they would await his pleasure and seek to beg him the favour of a small strip of land.

And so Adam Haveragh and his mother made their way by carrier's cart on the old highway from Washburndale to Knaresborough, crossing Oak Beck by the stone bridge, and finding their way over the desolate heath of Haregate Head, one day destined to become the site of a famous and fashionable spa, to reach the old town of Knaresborough high above the River Nidd.

It was Market Day and Adam and his mother had to push their way through a jostling throng. It was difficult, on crutches, to fight one's way past stall-holders selling a wide variety of wares - oatcakes, dried fish, sweet-meats, spices, salt, basketware, pottery, each stall crowded with buyers, by-standers, pickpockets. In the centre of the crowded market place a juggler

'...finding their way over the desolate heath of Haregate Head ... to reach the old town of Knaresborough.'

held court, whirling coloured balls in the air. A dancing bear, muzzled, was moving heavily to the beating of its owner's tambourine. A ballad-singer was hawking his wares. Pigs were squealing, geese honking.

They struggled through the crowd towards the forbidding entrance of the castle.

Already, other people were there - beggars, supplicants, a blind man, a wife with four children deserted by her husband. They joined the unhappy crowd, and waited. Minutes passed, an hour, then two. By now the crowd had grown to a score or more, the weak, the poor, the lame, the afflicted.

At last the castle gates were opened and two armed retainers appeared, each with a whip in his hand, brutally, callously clearing a path for the procession. The crowd cowered back and an old man, whose face had caught the whip end, whimpered.

They saw him for one brief second, the great John of Gaunt, as he came out on horseback, a powerful, handsome man dressed in red velvet and gold, on a fine white stallion.

But the prince, not heeding them, merely rode forward, urging his horse past the crowd. Several more retainers, also armed, followed.

The last, a steward paused to hurl a small handful of coins on the ground. The supplicants fell upon them, like a flock of pigeons after grain, scrabbling on the ground to grasp the coins in their fingers.

Adam and his mother, horrified, held back from the fray.

But the widow grasped the coat of the steward as he rode past.

'What do you want?' he said, evidently irritated.

'If you please,' said the widow, 'we wish to seek an audience with the prince.'

The steward, a haughty individual, was clearly shocked at the woman's forwardness, but he was determined to play along with her, to see how far she would go.

'And, pray, why should the prince seek audience with you?' he asked in a voice heavy with sarcasm.

'Oh, if you please, sir,' continued the widow, oblivious to the reality of the situation, 'we beg favour, my son and I, of some land.'

'Land?' said the steward, incredulous. 'You seek land?'

By now, a group of bystanders had gathered around, obviously enjoying the spectacle.

'Why, sir, yes,' said the woman, holding her hands out to him as if in prayer.

'Is that all,' said the steward. 'Forgive me, matron. I thought you were asking for something simple, like a piece of the moon.' And, hugely amused at his joke, he thrust the widow from him and roared with laughter as he rode away, leaving the crowd mocking the widow and her son. The crowd, pushed forward, knocking them to the ground, taunting them, leaving them lying in the dust.

'If ah could've only spoken to the prince,' said Adam as they made their way back in the carrier's cart which was now loaded with great sacks of grain, from the Plain of York, and a couple of piglets who, roughly tied by the trotters, lay on the floor of the cart and squealed piteously.

But when they reached the cottage, they were both depressed. It all seemed hopeless.

* * * * *

And yet, only a few weeks later, fate determined otherwise. It was a hot day in early June. Adam was outside, in the forest, gathering sticks, which he could only do painfully slowly, to bundle together as firewood. As each bundle was complete, he would fasten it round his shoulders and with it make a slow journey back to the cottage. They would use the firewood in the hearth or barter it for meat or a few eggs with neighbours.

As he came into a little clearing, he found himself standing face to face with Prince John of Gaunt, Duke of Lancaster.

The prince had obviously become separated from his party in the Royal Hunt and was resting in the warm sunlight, having dismounted. The hunting horns could be heard not far away.

'My Lord,' said Adam, struggling to find words. 'Forgive me, I can't...'

'Of course,' said the Prince, realising the cripple's embarrassment at being unable to bow or offer appropriate salutation to a man of his rank.

'Tell me, young man, how it came to pass that you lost the use of your limbs.'

And so Adam explained to him, as best he could, how his accident had happened. By now other members of the hunting party had joined them, and seeing the prince in conversation, hung back, waiting behind their master. Among them was the haughty steward who seemed not to recognise the supplicant of some weeks ago.

'I am sorry to hear of your misfortune,' said the prince. 'Were it in my power to help you, I most certainly would, but not the finest doctors in the land can return the power of your limbs.'

'But, sire, you can help me,' said Adam.

'Sire, if I had just a little land, I could earn enough to keep my mother and I.'

'But why should I give you land? Land has to be earned - in battle or by work.'

'Alas, sire, I can do neither.'

'What is your name?'

'Haveragh, sire, Adam de Haveragh.'

'Such is the name of the Park in the Forest that is my own' said the prince. 'So, just as I am John of Lancaster, you are Adam of Haveragh.' The hunters, sensing a jest, laughed.

'Aye, sir,' said Adam.

The prince mused. There was something about this lad, his honest, open manner, which appealed to him.

'How far, Adam, can you hop in a day?'

'I know not, sir. About five miles, perhaps.'

'I'll set you a challenge, Adam. If you can race the sun, on a long summer's day, the full eight miles around the outside of the Park, you can have the land, rent free for life.'

'Sire!'

Adam flung down his crutches and lay at the prince's feet. The others gasped their astonishment.

It was a formidable challenge. The eight miles consisted of rough waste, forest, moorland, bog - tough going for an able-bodied man; for a cripple a momentous challenge. And it had to be completed in a few hours.

The longest day of the year, St. Barnabas' Day, was chosen. Then the sun rose before four and wouldn't set until after ten, leaving over eighteen hours for the test.

Three judges would be selected for the race. One was a priest; another an attorney; the third the haughty attendant. They would begin the race as the sun rose above Norwood, starting from the little hunting lodge at Park Top, to this very day known as John o' Gaunt's Castle, and follow the ditch and wall for the full eight miles around the Park perimeter. The finishing point would be a high wall which divided that part of the forest from the park.

The day of the race came and, fortunately, it was a cool, misty morning, promising a fine day. Adam kissed his mother farewell and made his way to the appointed start where the judges were already waiting. They strained to see the sun rise and as the east began to lighten, they gave the signal and Adam began his race against the sun.

At first it was easy. The ground was smooth, with few trees in the way, and he could swing his body along in long, looping strides. After the first hour he had covered a good two miles and the task seemed an easy one.

But then he reached the first bog. His crutches sank almost waist deep in inky black mire and he floundered around, trying to find somewhere to pass. It was against the terms of the race to offer him help. For what seemed ages he struggled in the mud, moving only yards at a time before getting impossibly stuck. At one point he actually fell into the evil mire, struggled to recover himself, covered with mud. Every yard seemed to take an age. The bog seemed interminable.

At last he hauled himself onto higher land. But it had taken him nearly three hours to cover that horrendous mile.

Now he was dropping down a steep slope, the going difficult, slippery. Once his crutch slipped and he floundered across a muddy hillside, only regaining his position with difficulty.

It was now mid-morning and the sun was rising in the sky. He stumbled and slithered down the ravine to reach the Oak Beck, stopping to drink the water and wash the mud off himself. Then came the steep climb up the other side. Several times he had to crawl up the hillside, dragging his crutches behind him.

As the day wore on, he felt his strength subside. By now the sun was burning hot in the sky. His hands were sore, his shoulders ached. Ahead lay another area of bog.

Precious time was lost as he floundered around once again. At one time a crutch became hopelessly stuck in the morass and there seemed no way of pulling it free. By now a crowd of spectators had gathered and one of them offered to rush forward to help him retrieve the crutch but the judges restrained him. Any help whatsoever would disqualify him; on that subject the attorney was quite certain. So Adam struggled on, moving painfully slowly.

Now came a great area of dense scrubland, of bramble and gorse. The judges, all men of mature years but able-bodied, complained bitterly at even following him as the spines and prickles clung to their cloaks. Wearily, now suffering real pain from sore hands, Adam battled on, hacking his way forward.

Time ticked by. Progress was agonisingly slow. People began to look up at the sky. A long afternoon was turning to a fine, gentle evening. Shadows were lengthening and the little figure could be seen now moving a single pace forward, then stopping to recover strength and breath. Time was running out. Could he still make it?

He was pale, exhausted, close to collapse with the sheer effort of it all. He was scratched and his hands sore to bleeding.

They saw him collapse, motionless with exhaustion, then drag himself along a few more bitterly-fought yards.

The sun was sinking. There was still a mile to go.

From somewhere he found, within himself, unknown reserves of determination and energy. He struggled forward.

Mercifully, on the higher land, the going was easier. He kept moving, oblivious of the pain and the tiredness, shoulders heaving the two sticks forward, feeble legs pivoting. In the west, the sun was sinking towards the high ridge of the darkening fells. It would be all over in minutes. Gritting his teeth, his face contorted with effort and with pain, Adam made his final thrust. The sun was now little more than a thin, orange line above the fell. Ahead was the final wall. He swung, frantic. A crowd had gathered in the evening light.

He swung his body forward, again and again. The last few seconds slipped away as the sun began to vanish. The wall was just yards away. He flung himself at it.

The sun was almost gone. To complete the course he had to get over the wall. It was no more than six feet high, a simple scramble and leap for an able-bodied man. But for Adam it was beyond all endurance. Desperate, as the light vanished, he flung his two crutches over the wall and they clattered across the other side as he collpased into exhaustion.

But had he done it? Had he won the race against the sun?

The crowd turned to the three judges who, white-faced themselves, now must take the crucial decision.

'No!' said the attorney. 'The terms of the race are that his feet must touch the point where he started.'

The crowd groaned.

'Nonsense!' cried the priest. 'In the eyes of God and therefore of man, his crutches are his feet, therefore he has won!'

The crowd shouted its approval.

But now it lay to the final judge, the arogant courtier, to have the casting vote. Alarmed, he turned round. Standing behind him was the prince himself. He looked into the prince's eyes.

'He has WON!'

A roar of delight from the crowd. The cripple was carried aloft. There was feasting and celebration right into the night.

* * * * *

John of Lancaster kept his promise. Adam was made master of Haveragh Park and all rights and incomes thereto appertaining, which meant, in plain words, he was charged with the breeding of the prince's and the king's horses and deer. He became a man of rank, a loyal servant of the prince and able manager of the estate. He learned to ride a horse side-saddle and often took his aged mother on rides across the Park. They would often canter up to Scargill top, above the winding course of the Oak Beck, from where they could see the estate and the long line of ditch and wall where, so long ago, he had pursued that desperate race against the sun.

The Shepherd Lord

The boy watched the two gentlemen riding through the village. They were not from these parts, that was sure. He looked at their silk stockings, slashed silk doublets, cloaks of finest velvet, caps with curling feathers. City men, not dressed for travelling through the Cumberland fells. They were hesitating, as if they had lost their way. Seeing the lad, they approached him.

'Is this Threlkeld village, boy?'

'Aye,' replied the lad, noncommittal.

'Could you tell me which is Thistlethwaite's farm?'

'Yon.' A lad of few words, he indicated a low, thatched building at the far end of the town. A farmhouse.

The two men rode over to the cottage, dismounted and hammered on the door. An old woman appeared.

'Is this the home of Will Thistlethwaite, Farmer?'

'He died,' said the old woman. 'Two year sin. Would yer want to speak to my son?'

'We do indeed,' said the traveller.

'He's up ont' fell,' said the old woman. 'But 'happen he'll be back any time now. You'd best come in.'

The boy was summoned to hold the horses and, for his pains, was given a penny piece. The boy couldn't help noticing their perfectly starched ruffs and a faint whiff of perfume.

The house was a simple one. Even though it was a mild early September afternoon, a peat fire glowed in the ingle-nook. There was a scrubbed table, two or three chairs and a stool. Great hams hung curing from hooks on the ceiling joists.

'Perhaps we should explain who we are,' said the traveller, who so far had been spokesman. 'My name is Sir Percival Lawrence and this is Giles Fletcher, my clerk and attorney.'

'Pleased to meet you, I'm sure,' said the old woman in tones that were deferential. 'Can I give you a little ale to drink?'

A large pot jug and pewter mugs were produced from the kitchen. The men, tired after their journey on dry and dusty roads, drank.

'Thank you kindly, Madam,' said Sir Percival.

'Henry'll be here soon,' said the old woman, apprehensively. 'He's allus here before the church clock strikes six.'

The two men looked round the simple cottage, evidently startled at its austerity. There was a noise outside.

The door burst open. A tall, well-built man in his early thirties filled the door-frame. He was carrying a half-grown, injured lamb over his shoulders.

'Nah then,' he said evidently surprised. 'We've visitors. A pair of fine horses, Mother, Ah-' he saw the two travellers and was silent, his mouth open.

Sir Percival rose.

'Henry de Clifford, Lord of Westmorland and Skipton, I greet you in the name of His Majesty, King Henry VII.'

The young man looked startled. He took the lamb from his shoulders and laid it on the ground.

'Nay - nay - tha's got it wrong. Ah'm Henry Thistlethwaite, shepherd to Sir Launcelot Threlkeld, a true knight. Ah'm...' he looked round nervously, as if he might flee.

'Fear not, brave Clifford,' interposed Giles Fletcher. 'Have you not heard of the death of King Richard III on Bosworth field?'

'And crowning of Henry Tudor to be King Henry, Seventh of that name of England?' continued Sir Percival.

'-thus restoring the fortunes of Lancaster?' added Fletcher.

The old woman was on her knees, crossing herself before Henry.

'Indeed 'tis true,' she said. 'That Almighty God has let me see this day! Long, long years ago we swore a solemn oath, your father and I, never to tell the secret of your birth. Will Thistlethwaite took that secret to his grave, but the Good Lord has spared me to live to see this day.'

Bewildered, the young shepherd sat on the nearest chair.

'It nivver is...'

Sir Percival turned to the young man.

'You must forgive us. Lady Margaret has, in fact, told us that she kept the full truth of your high birth from you in case your father's enemies should find you and extract it from you under duress.'

'So, let me explain to you, as briefly as I can, the circumstances of your birth. Your father was Lord John De Clifford, a great soldier but a man of fierce disposition, who died a soldier's death before the Battle of Towton in 1761.

'He lost more than his life. His estates and property were taken from your mother, you and your brother when your father was attainted. You and your brother were in immediate peril of your lives, in part, to revenge the death of the young Duke of Rutland whom your father's enemies claim he had killed. Be that as it may, your mother, realising the peril you were in, despatched you to Cumberland and your brother, Richard, to Holland where, alas, he soon perished. Her instructions were that the secret of your birth should be kept from everyone in the world, even from you yourself and these good people, who brought you up as a shepherd lad, were to claim you as their own true son.'

Henry Clifford, who had been listening with gaping mouth, now rose.

'I remember - travelling, battles, rumours, being brought here, being told that these good people were now my true mother and father and never to think or to remember, on pain of death, all that had gone before.'

'You were seven years of age when you were brought here to begin a new life. Almost twenty-five years ago,' said Sir Percival.

'It's true, as I live,' said the old woman. 'Lady Margaret is your true mother. She has denied herself all these long years, for fear and love of you.'

Clifford held his head in his hands. So - the days when Lady Margaret and Sir Launcelot had called at this cottage, or summoned him to the big house, they had known everything but dare not speak to him. So - Will and Eliza Thistlewaite had merely fostered him. How much they had done for him! It was suddenly too much - a wave of emotion overcame him. He seized the old woman in his powerful arms.

'Tha's allus mother to me,' he said.

Giles Fletcher coughed nervously.

'The King is anxious that your rightful estates be returned to you, but before this can be done we must present a petition to His Majesty. A mere formality, I do assure you. But unless he receives such a document we are powerless to act. Lord Clifford, we need your signature to this document.'

From his bag he produced a scroll and unfastening the ribbon around it, presented it to Clifford. Clifford unrolled it.

'Nay,' he said, sheepishly. 'Ah canna understand letters.'

There was an embarrassed silence.

'Of course,' said Sir Percival. 'Your mother's instructions kept to the letter. You were to be brought up exactly as a shepherd lad. Please may I read it?'

It was a long and lengthy legal document beginning 'In most humble and lowly wise I beseech your Highness -' and containing many 'therefores' and legal terms and pleadings.

'Ah can't make head nor tail on't,' protested Henry Clifford.

'In this you must respect your family's legal advisers. It is important that the King receives such a document so that it may be clearly demonstrated that the land and property which are yours are indeed rightfully and properly due to you.'

'How much property is there?'

Fletcher took another piece of parchment from his bag. He then began a lengthy description of lands and castles, farms and water mills and sundry other items throughout the length and breadth of Westmorland and Yorkshire.

'That's half England.'

'Not quite,' said Sir Percival. 'But it makes you one of the richest and most powerful men in the North.'

'But we need your signature on this document before we can present it on your behalf,' said Fletcher. He then added, as an afterthought, 'you can write?'

'Nay - ah dunna ken,' said Clifford. 'But ah can spell me name.'

Fletcher produced a quill pen and a tiny bottle of ink. The scroll was laid on the table and slowly, carefully, with his tongue out, Henry Clifford wrote the name 'Henry' in bold, firm strokes. But as he began to shape a 'T' he stopped.

'Laws - ah can only spell "Thistlethwaite". But tha' tells me mi name isna "Thistlethwaite" onny more'.

'Good heavens, of course,' realised Fletcher, and carefully he held Clifford's hand as the C and the L, I and two FFs, an O, an R and a D were written.

'You'll have to practice that. You'll be needing it quite a lot.'

Sir Percival now informed Clifford he was to travel with them at least as far as Skipton Castle. There was no time to lose. They were due to meet Sir Launcelot and Lady Margaret at the Hall before starting their journey next day at dawn.

'But ah canna go in all me muck. 'Ah've nowt to wear.'

'That'll be taken care of,' said Sir Percival.

So Henry, Tenth Lord of the Honour of Skipton and of Westmorland, washed himself at the village pump and put on his cleanest old clothes, until more suitable garments were ready for him, before travelling to see his natural mother and begin a journey through his newly inherited estates.

But he bade good Eliza Thistlethwaite a long and tearful farewell and promised, when all the papers were presented and he was the master of his lands, she should be given a fine house in a splendid country estate.

'Nay, lad,' she said, 'Ah'm nivver goin' away fra where ah belong.'

Lady Margaret, decorously dressed in black, now silver-haired and frail, greeted her son. They ate together for the first time for a quarter of a century and she explained to him how she had had to lie in so many ways to convince him he had not been her son. Only by that denial, terrible though the sacrifice had been, could she have ensured the spies sent to kill him would not guess his whereabouts.

But as the old lady listened to his guttural dialect and noticed his thick, muscular, shepherd's hands, she realised that, in more than one essential sense, he had now become another's son. But at least she, too, had been spared to see this happy day.

Clothes suitable for a great gentleman were soon found and next day Clifford set out with Sir Percival and Fletcher and a group of retainers, on the journey south to Yorkshire. Almost every estate had a castle - Brougham, Brough, Appleby and Pendragon and Skipton itself. Wherever they trav-

'After several days travel they came to Skipton.'

elled local people, tenant farmers, servants, came out to greet them, curtseying, shaking him warmly by the hand.

And they were surprised and delighted to meet someone who talked the language of the common people - could talk about farming, the harvest, haytime, sheep, and the weather. He was one of them.

But at the fine castles he was more confused. The rooms were vast and cold, the beds uncomfortable. The food was so rich his stomach revolted. And he was not a good horseman, riding but occasionally, more used to tramping the fells on foot behind his flock.

After several days' travel they came to Skipton. Sir Percival and Fletcher left for the Court where the petition was to be presented to the King. Clifford was to stay in Skipton where he was given the most commodious rooms in the tower and the staff, until recently in liege to King Richard III himself, were told to welcome the restoration of their ancestral Lord with singing, dancing, music and feasting - activities which went on in the old High Street of Skipton - a special fair arranged with jugglers and dancing bears.

But all the while, Henry Clifford was deeply miserable. He had acquired greatness and fortune but had lost his native fells, his sheep; he was in a world he neither cared for nor understood, of obsequious servants and fawning lackeys, a host of supplicants begging favours. He would have none of it.

'My Lord, will you join us on the hunt?' enquired the Chief Steward.

It seemed a better prospect than the gloomy castle and so he joined a group of horsemen and falconers on the chase through the park behind the Norman Castle, over the wide expanse of Barden Moor, famous for its fine red deer.

They would take food at Barden Tower, an old hunting lodge by the River Wharfe. As they rode over the fell and down into the valley this, for Henry Clifford, was one of the most entrancing sights of his life. There the Wharfe curved through a steep-sided, richly-wooded dale, already beginning to acquire the yellows and golds of autumn and the hunting lodge, situated on a bluff above the river, in a woodland clearance, offered a vision of paradise. It reminded him of his Lakeland home, the peace and tranquility his nature yearned. Here he would return and here he would live when he had the power and authority to do so.

And so it came about. He appointed able, competent and trusting people who were soon to learn that their young lord had all a countryman's native wit and shrewdness They were to look after the great castles at Brough, Skipton and Appleby whilst he chose to live with a small group of retainers in the peace and tranquility of Barden.

But something else was troubling him. He sent a message to the Prior of nearby Bolton Priory and early one morning a young monk, Brother Gilbert, presented himself at the gates of Barden Tower.

'You sent for me, my Lord?'

'Brother, I wish you to teach me - to write and to read, to master mathematics and philosophy, astronomy and the mysteries of our Lord and of our earth.'

And so, from that day forward, the monk could be seen coming to Barden each day with books and manuscripts in a travelling bag.

Clifford was a quick, able and enthusiastic scholar, making up for lost years by energy, enthusiasm and natural flair. When it came to astronomy, he soon proved the value of a shepherd's knowledge, knew full well the Plough and the Great Bear from nights of lonely contemplation on the fellside. His teachers were astonished. He knew of plants and herbs and could identify healing herbs, and showed intense interest in the new science of alchemy.

Soon his reputation as a scholar grew and learned men came to see him. Treatises were sent to Barden and his ability to absorb and comment on them was considered among the most remarkable of the age.

Nor did the Shepherd Lord neglect his estates or wider affairs of state. He was regarded by his tenants and all who knew him as a wise and just man, capable of acting firmly. He was summoned to Court, where he was seen as a 'quiet country gentleman', unused to the ways of the Royal Palace but a loyal supporter of the King. He married Anne, daughter of Sir John St. John, a distant relative of the King himself. In his sixtieth year he supported his monarch by leading a force of fighting men from Wharfedale and Craven in the great battle against the Scots at Flodden Field where, though not a natural fighting man, he acquitted himself with honour. One of the pikes carried by his men at Flodden is kept, to this very day, in the little Upper Wharfedale Museum in Grassington.

Yet, to his last days, he remained a solitary man. The death of his wife and the dissolute behaviour of his son darkened his life.

To the end, a Dalesman passing Barden Tower and seeing a grey-haired figure standing outside Barden Tower staring across at the wide open fell, lost in contemplation and reliving the freedom of his boyhood years, would turn to his companion and say:

'It's nobbut t' Shepherd Lord.'

The Nut Brown Maid

Slowly, with deep chests heaving, the horses carrying the little party struggled up the steep mountain track, the lead-horse reaching the top of the brow as the last one was only part way up the final slope.

'We must rest the horses awhile,' said Burgess, Chief Steward, to his companion as the younger man, on the lead-horse, turned to him. There were eleven in the party - three women and eight men. The women, who rode side-saddle, were inconspicuously, if elegantly, dressed; the men, evidently servants and retainers, were all armed. It was a warm afternoon in late May, the unexpected heat after a cold spring making travel uncomfortably hot.

Burgess looked back at the last horse which was carrying a heavily-built lady up the last few yards to the summit. The horses panted as the little group gathered.

Burgess looked up at the sun.

'At least another hour to Middleham,' he said.

'Perhaps more,' said Talbot, his companion, smiling down at the corpulent lady on her suffering horse. The two other women, much younger and far better horsewomen, had already joined them. Burgess turned to them.

'We must be out of these hills by nightfall,' he observed. The unspoken thought was of rumours that bands of robbers were hereabouts - outlaws living off the land and whatever could be taken from unfortunate travellers. He had advised Lady Margaret not to go this way, not to take the direct road from Skipton through Wharfedale and Coverdale. But she was a headstrong young woman, used to having her own way. They were returning from Chester where Lady Margaret had been visiting family friends. Having reached Skipton, Burgess had advocated the longer, but safer, route to Northumberland, by Otley and Knaresborough and along the Great North Road, rather than across these lonely hills. Lady Margaret, impatient as ever, wished to save a day and cut through the wild wastes of the Dales direct to Middleham and then on via Richmond.

They had, of course, taken all necessary precautions. The men were all well trained and well armed, they were dressed plainly like simple travellers and carried with them only the minimum of gold and valuables. Given the beauty of the weather, with the trees of the Dales newly breaking into leaf, and a cloudless blue sky overhead, the journey seemed easy and safe enough.

And so they had followed the busy market road from Skipton to Rylstone, calling to see the Nortons of Rylstone Hall, old friends of the family, where they had spent the night before continuing their journey through Linton and Threshfield, Kilnsey and Kettlewell and on to the murderously steep pass over Park Rash. A somewhat extended stop at the inn in Kettlewell had taken up more of the afternoon than planned and their progress over the pass into Coverdale had been very slow. Burgess was responsible to the earl for his daughter's safe journey and he would not rest easy until they were safe on Percy lands.

Burgess looked round. Even Lady Margaret's plump chaperone looked ready to continue, so he gently urged his horse forward, the ascent now easy as the way flattened out. They were crossing into Coverdale over the shoulder of Great Whernside mountain. Soon, on the left, they passed a tall, single stone, the Hunter Stone, a prominent waymark by the roadside to guide travellers. The track made its way above a shallow ravine, the start of Coverdale then, as now, a wild, bleak area but in those days covered by scattered woodland, mainly birch trees. This, thought Burgess, was the place of greatest risk, the ravine and the tree cover where men of villainous purpose could be concealed.

Yet, with the white birch trunks and fine, patterned leaves dappling the light as they began the descent into Cover Beck, nothing could seem more benign than this wood. Hazels, too, were breaking into leaf, whole banks of fresh new green covering the hillside ahead. Burgess relaxed on his saddle.

At the bottom of the slope the track suddenly switchbacked into the hillside to cross a little ravine formed by Hem Gill Beck, but as the party came round the corner someone was waiting for them.

It all happened with lightening speed. The only thing that Burgess remembered was a weight thrust at his back, a gloved hand over his mouth toppling him violently from his horse, crashing him to the ground. He struggled in vain. Before he could recover his senses, his sword had been taken from him and his own dagger was pointing at his throat. Amid the scuffling around him women were shrieking.

It had been an ambush, brilliantly executed. They had obviously observed the party coming and had chosen the exact point to take advantage of cover and the steep hillside making the most of surprise. Each assailant had chosen a victim.

Within moments, outmanoeuvred and outnumbered, the party was captured, each of the men bound and trussed like a chicken. Only one retainer, Talbot, had managed even to draw a sword and his gashed hand, bleeding profusely, bore witness to the hopelessness of the struggle.

The women, too, had been forced to dismount and each was firmly held by a bearded ruffian who made them wince with pain every time they attempted to struggle.

They eyed their captors.

There were a score, perhaps, of raggedly dressed, unshaven or bearded men, some no more than boys. Their appearance was filthy, more like beggars than peasants. Yet their eyes were wild, exultant at the capture of their prey.

The horses were gathered and led away and the travellers bunched together by their captors. The men, with their hands bound behind them, were dragged on a length of rope like dancing bears; the women were thrust into the middle of a circle of jeering and grimacing faces.

'Your purses, if you please,' said the leader of the band, a youth, judging by his fresh face and soft young beard, scarce two or three-and-twenty. Yet his voice was not that of a street-beggar or vagrant. He spoke in cultivated tones.

Lady Margaret looked at his dress. Old and torn by rough wear and usage, yet the boots had been of fine quality, the doublet, for all it was torn and stained, carefully tailored.

'Take what you will,' said Burgess, defiantly. 'You'll find little for your trouble.'

One of the band went round each of them, knife in hand, lifting a doublet to locate a purse, cutting it off, throwing it into a central pile. The women were treated in the same way and Lady Margaret recoiled as the robber approached her. The man stank. Her little leather purse was cut from its thong, cast into the heap.

'Rich pickings indeed', said the leader, with a smile.

'You'll pay for this with your life!' exclaimed Burgess. The robber turned to him and plucked him by the beard until he winced.

'That'll depend on who lives to tell the tale,' he responded, taking his dagger from its sheath and holding it menacingly close to Burgess' throat. Burgess spat. In a flash two powerful blows to the stomach had Burgess rolling on the ground in agony.

'Brute!'

The robber turned to his accuser. Lady Margaret, aware of the risk she had run, did not flinch. He looked at her rich brown hair flowing in tresses.

'Those were foolish words my pretty little Nut Brown Maid,' said the robber. 'You should know what happens to pretty little Nut Brown Maids.'

He stepped close to her, leant forward and kissed her. She slapped him fiercely across the cheek, leaving a hand-mark which quickly reddened. Men leapt from behind her and grasped her arms until her eyes filled with tears of pain.

'Wildcat!' The young man rubbed his cheek.

Suddenly the older woman, Lady Margaret's travelling companion and chaperone, thrust herself forward.

'Villain,' she cried. 'Don't you realise that you are addressing the daughter of a noble earl? You will pay for this with your life. Don't you know how to treat a great lady?'

The robber-leader looked at Lady Margaret and paused a moment. Here was a great opportunity. If she was a daughter of a great and famous family, there could be ransom money. But this could also be a dangerous game.

'Then who, pray, are you, Nut Brown Maid?'

Lady Margaret remained silent, aloof.

'Shall I make her talk?' said the man holding her. Margaret winced as he tightened his grip.

'No. Release her. We are men of honour. A lady in our company shall be treated with all the dignity and courtesy her womanhood deserves.'

He gazed at her. She was of medium height with pale skin, delicate features and rich, auburny-brown hair which fell around her shoulders above her riding hood.

'My lady, tell me who you are.'

Silence.

It was the other young woman, Margaret's companion, her maid, who spoke.

'My Lady is no other than Lady Margaret Percy, daughter of the great Earl of Northumberland.'

A gasp of astonishment went through the crowd. A daughter of the Percies in their capture - here in Coverdale. Comments, some of them ribald, passed through the robber band.

The young robber-leader in an instant saw the danger of his position. The Percies were the greatest and most powerful family in the North. Once they heard of this misdemeanour he would be hunted like the wild deer, caught and quartered without mercy by a Percy sword. What had seemed at first sight like a merchant and his family, an easy picking, now had turned into a dangerous snare. Whether he killed or released his prey, Percy vengeance would fall.

'Silence!' he called, and the robbers' ribaldry ceased.

He stepped forward to Lady Margaret and, to the astonishment of captives and captors alike, went down on his knee and, before she could resist, took and kissed her hand.

'Lady, I pray you be our guest and stay a while in our greenwood haunts.'

'That cannot be, sir,' said Lady Margaret. 'I beg you to release us immediately, return our purses and let us continue our journey.'

Murmurs of discontent came from behind. The young man would have to play his cards carefully. His band would have their spoils. He must play for time.

'I would dearly wish to release you, my Lady,' he explained. 'But my good men must be paid for their troubles -'

'Aye,' said a voice from the rear.

'- and what is to prevent you reaching Middleham Castle and there raising the alarm to bring armed men to hunt us out of these our hills?'

'Aye, that we shall indeed,' interposed Burgess. 'Each and every one of you will hang from the nearest oak tree.'

'Unless we put paid to your prattling tongue first!' rejoined the robber-leader. 'Corpses, I recall, buried in a deep grave cannot give secrets away. So, dear Lady, as you see we are each other's prisoner. Will you accept our poor hospitality?'

'You give me no choice, sir,' she said.

'Do we have your word that you will not attempt to escape or to flee?'

'You do,' she said.

So the prisoners were untied and, under discreet armed guard, were taken along the track, soon branching off up the hillside through the woodland. Margaret's horse was returned and she was allowed to ride alongside the robber-leader.

Now that immediate risk of violence had receded she began to collect her thoughts. There was indeed something strange about her captor, something connected to the rumours she had heard. It was time to play a careful game.

'Perhaps you would tell me your name, sir, now that you know who I am?' she asked innocently.

'I would like to, my Lady, but think of me as just an outlaw.'

'You must have a name.'

'Then call me Harry.'

She looked at him carefully. He was an attractive man, with a strong, manly bearing and interesting eyes. He had the slender hands of an aristocrat and carried himself with dignity. His clothes, though old, were worn with elegance. In spite of herself she found herself fascinated by him.

She was aware he was returning the glance and felt herself blushing.

'My Lady, I -'

She turned away and urged her horse forward, trembling.

They came to a clearing. Ahead was what appeared to be a camp site, close to a steep ravine cutting down the fellside. Built against the fellside was a low hut of timber, its roof thatched with moorland ling and turfs.

'Welcome to our little encampment.'

They dismounted. For a moment she stood, holding the horse's reins. He approached her, those handsome eyes pools of darkness. Something inside her snapped. He was kissing her passionately. Waves of emotion like flashes of lightning ran through her. She could hear voices as others approached and pushed herself free.

'You insult me, sir,' she said, without conviction.

'My Nut-brown maid...'

'My Lady, are you all right?' came the voice of her protectress. Anxiously, the woman forced herself forward to her ward's side.

'Leave me be,' Margaret responded sharply. 'I have this gentleman's word for my safe conduct and protection.'

'How can you believe - ?'

'Pray hold your tongue!'

She turned to Harry.

'I ask you, sir, to make all necessary provision for my servants and retainers.'

'Gladly, my Lady.'

A fire was quickly lit and the hut made ready to receive the guests. But when Margaret peered inside she was overwhelmed by its stench.

'The place is only fit for beasts!'

An outlaw was set to work clearing out the filth and fresh reeds and bracken were laid were on the floor and simple beds made up. But Margaret vowed she would not sleep there. She would rather sleep on the greensward and have the stars for a counterpane.

It was soon dusk. By now, hunks of venison and wild boar were being turned on spits over the fire. The group gathered round to receive portions of meat served with oatcake, as flagons of rough ale and stolen wine were being passed around. Tensions eased as the alcohol flowed and even the captured retainers forgot their wounds and the disgrace of their situation as great chunks of juicy meat and oatcake were devoured by the light of the fire. Someone was playing a lute, its notes melancholy across the night-time air. Even the two other women, taking their cue from Margaret, decided to make the best of the situation and soon retired to the beds offered in the hut.

Most of the men, drunken almost to a stupor, friend and foe now, at least for this night, reconciled made a rough bivouac among the trees.

Only the robber-leader and Lady Margaret lay awake as the fire sank to its embers. Gradually she had begun to unravel his secrets, hear of his education, his knowledge of the court of his namesake, King Harry. There was more to find out. But now he was questioning her.

'Could you fall in love with an outlaw?'

'It is possible.'

'If you did, could you sacrifice everything for a life of vagrancy and live with him in the greenwood, hunting the red deer, risking capture, disgrace and hanging?'

'If I loved him enough I would cut my hair short, roll up my skirts and learn to shoot a longbow as straight and accurate as any man to bring down the deer and to defend the one I loved.'

'You'd cut that beautiful hair?'

'It is possible.'

'And you'd face disgrace and dishonour for the man you loved?'

'Even if my mother wept for shame, and that would be hard to bear, I'd do it for the man I love.'

'Even if you knew that the man had had another woman?'

'If I loved him enough, that wouldn't matter to me.'

'Could you love me enough?'

She looked at him. The firelight gilded his face. She saw the earnestness, the intensity of his expression. In spite of herself she leant forward and touched his hand.

'Then I would ask you to be true to me and to tell me who you really are.'

'But I ask you to love me as a penniless outlaw whose corpse must one day swing in the wind.'

'I love you.'

Tears filled his eyes. She continued.

'Then tell me, my love, who are you?'

He paused.

'My name is Harry de Clifford, my father is Lord Clifford, Lord of Skipton and Westmorland.'

'The Shepherd Lord.'

'He disowned me. I led a life of wildness and extravagance - the folly of youth. I had wealth enough from my father and grew up with young Prince Harry, and at court, deceived and cheated by the ways of the world, tried to live to those same standards when he became King. My father took exception to my extravagance. When I returned to Yorkshire with an elegant suit and a bridle-cover of cloth-of-gold we quarrelled violently and I insulted his servants. He complained to the king and threw me out of the house.

'So I had to fend for myself. I took to the woods with a group of tavern friends and we live by wickedness. I confess it all to you. We rob travellers, attack farmhouses, even whole villages - the villagers are forced to shelter in the church when we loot and pillage.

'There's no way out. Sooner or later we'll be captured and hanged.'

He hurled a faggot into the fire. The flames leapt, consuming it. 'Perhaps if Margaret had lived...'

'Margaret?'

'My wife. I married at twenty. She was only eighteen. But she died carrying our first -'

He became silent. She watched him.

'You're also Margaret.'

'Don't expect me to -' she began.

'What?' he asked.

'I was going to say "save you"'

'I would do anything for you.'

'The River Wharfe, peat-brown and dark, flowed beneath their feet as they crossed the narrow bridge at Barden...and climbed the hill to Barden Tower.'

'Would you go with me, tomorrow, to your father, and beg his forgiveness?'

'No. I couldn't, he'd -'

'Then I can do nothing for you.'

'I thought you said you loved me.' He turned away gloomily. 'So I'll be betrayed, hanged, and you'll quickly forget, find another.'

'Then come with me.'

'If I do, will you be mine?'

For answer she leaned across and kissed him, tenderly.

They slept by the fire embers, as innocently as children, pressed together by warmth. At dawn they arose and woke the others. He issued orders.

The prisoners were to be released, immediately, their purses and goods restored. The robber-band was instructed to go into hiding. The former captives pledged to keep their secret.

Margaret and Harry Clifford rode alone next day, retracing their journey back over Coverdale, Park Rash and Wharfedale, following the Dale downriver to Barden.

Once again the weather was magnificent and the beauty of the fells seemed to rejoice in their happiness. The River Wharfe, peat-brown and dark, flowed beneath their feet as they crossed the narrow bridge at Barden. They climbed the hill to Barden Tower, dismounted and left their horses in the little courtyard. It was a rich, golden afternoon.

A servant answered the door.

'Lord Harry - how good to see you.'

Margaret stepped forward.

'Please, tell Lord Clifford that Lady Margaret Percy and a companion are here to see him.'

Lord Clifford was in his study, the room littered with papers of astrology and alchemy. His fame as a scholar and philosopher had spread wide. But, as he rose to greet his guests, his face darkened.

'Villain!'

Margaret thrust herself forward.

'Lord Clifford, I, as daughter of the Earl of Northumberland, beseech you to take back to your heart your contrite and sorrowing son who comes to beg forgiveness both in his own and my name, who am his newly betrothed.'

Conflicting emotions crossed Lord Clifford's face. He took a step backwards, holding on to the great desk behind him.

'Is this true, Harry?'

Harry said nothing, but kneeled down on the rush strewn floor before his father. Margaret kneeled down with him.

The old man laid his hands on each of their heads, like a priest giving benediction. As they rose to their feet they saw that he was weeping and he kissed them.

'She has saved you from the gallows, Harry,' said the old Lord taking her hands in his. 'And more besides.'

'My Nut Brown Maid,' he said.

For the great and powerful, misdemeanour can easily be forgotten. In those lawless times and in that part of England, when the great families of the North held power, it was politic to forget the excesses of a youth who would one day become a pillar of the state. Only a ballad singer, learning of the tale, was to record its essence in a poem of wit and beauty.

Within a year Margaret bore a son, destined to continue the Clifford dynasty. The former outlaw succeeded his father as Eleventh Lord but was soon advanced by King Henry VIII to become the first Earl of Cumberland, one of a succession of men of that title who played a major part in the history of England.

And all for the love of a Nut Brown Maid!

Potter Thompson

There it stands—Richmond—perhaps the finest Castle in the North. Its impressive appearance on its great hilltop spur almost takes your breath away as you see it for the first time, coming over the long hill from Wensleydale. Alan the Red's tall keep seems to rise out of the very bedrock itself, those massive retaining walls looking as if they've always been there, as if they have grown out of the hard limestone, as the trees have grown. The trees, ash and thorn, ring the base of the rock on which the castle stands, their soft greens making a leafy and subtle contrast against the grey limestone. Below, in the rocky gorge of the Swale, the river's brown waters swirl and tumble, white and foaming against the boulders of the river bed.

If the castle seems to have taken root and grown out of the living rock, the town is something which has grown out of the castle itself, Saxon serfs seeking protection and patronage from their Norman overlords, the many crowded stables, taverns, workshops, alleyways, courtyards, a busy Market Place, two churches and, eventually, even a theatre to serve initially the garrison and then the important administrative and trading centre that Richmond town became.

The Market soon was a focal point of life—wool and knitted stockings from the thousands of black-faced Swaledale sheep, lead mined from the hills, all traded for corn from the plain and other necessities.

Fairs were held in Richmond Market Place and to this very day travelling showmen bring their fairground attractions to the people of Richmond—roundabouts with wooden horses, shooting galleries, penny arcades, stalls of every kind and variety, bright lights and music.

So who could blame a servant-girl at such a fair in Richmond town long, long ago, on a fine summer night when the light never seemed to want to fade from the sloping fields high above the town, from taking her companion, a dark-eyed fairground lad, away from the noise and bright lights to dally in the long grass of June? The gin that had burned her throat, his sharp-cut features, beautifully embroidered shirt of finest linen and his winning smile were poetry to overcome all resistance as she yielded to his caresses.

As he rose to leave her he took from around his neck a little gold cross and slipped it over her head, kissed her and seemed to blend into the dark shadows of the moonlit field.

She never saw him again. But Mary Thompson had cause enough to rue his visit. Before autumn was out it was obvious to all she was big with child.

Stoically she bore her shame and her sorrow and in Spring, in a dim attic attended only by an old woman she gave birth to a healthy boy. Alas for poor Mary she took a fever and in a few days time she died.

The boy grew up in the town orphanage. Dark, even swarthy in appearance, they called him 'Gypsy' or 'Potter' Thompson, and though baptised 'Peter' he knew no name but 'Potter'.

From his earliest days, Potter Thompson was marked as someone different from his street-urchin companions in both temperament and appearance. He was a quiet, introspective lad, considered by many to be a dreamer, and often ridiculed and bullied for his oddity. As he grew older and his muscles grew harder, he could more ably defend himself, and then could sometimes thrash his opponents. Indeed he was known for a temper so violent that once he smashed a bone in an opponent' s nose and was soundly beaten for his misdeeds by the parson.

As a man he didn' t change. He became a stone-mason, skilled at carving letters on gravestones or mileposts and, for a sovereign, would carve you a cherub or a sundial. But he remained a solitary figure, a tactiturn man who would sit over his tankard of ale for an hour or more without speaking, save to suck upon an old clay pipe.

He didn't marry. He once said he'd 'nowt to say to womenfolk' and no doubt it was because he was too shy.

Yet he wore the little gold cross around his neck, saved for him by the old woman who had been his mother's midwife, the link between the mother he had never known and the father of whomhe was equally oblivious.

And those that had teased him and mocked him when they were lads now had a grudging respect for him, both as a skilled workman and a 'deep 'un' who didn't waste a word.

And if he spent a little too much of his time on solitary walks around the town or even into the local countryside, that was only Potter Thompson's way.

They would watch him from Richmond Bridge, on the rocky footpath along the base of the rock on which the mighty castle stands. And if they saw him stand and stare deep into the waters of the River Swale, they thought nothing of it.

One such summer evening he took that favourite walk along that familiar path, every tree and stone known to him. He paused, as was his wont, and looked across at the river and then on an impulse turned round to gaze up at the steep grassy slope above him. Something caught his attention. Something odd. It was a dark patch just behind a gnarled ash tree growing out of a crevice. Like a cave. He had never noticed that before.

Intrigued, he scrambled forward up the hillside, along a vestigial rabbit path towards the ash tree. It was steep and he had to tread carefully. Sure

"Something caught his attention.......It was a dark patch just behind a gnarled ash tree grown out of a crevice. Like a cave."

enough, it was a dark crevice in the rock, a narrow cave, just wide enough for a slim man to squeeze into. Almost without thinking about it he stepped forward into the space, easing himself forward. He expected to feel damp rock or earth ahead, as the cave sloped to a dead end. But no—there was more space. Gingerly he stumbled forward, feeling his way with his feet and his arms, like a blind man. He took hesitant steps, now a little frightened, but unwilling to turn back. He took several more steps into the blackness.

Suddenly he was aware that the passage was opening out into a large space. His footsteps, his very breathing, seemed to echo. He was aware he was entering a larger cave.

Gradually, his eyes began to get used to the dark. His reason told him that this shouldn't be so, where there was absolute blackness he should see nothing. But this wasn't. He was aware of a faint grey light and space around him, as if he were standing in a great cave, like a huge church or chamber of the castle far above. Gradually his eyes could decipher forms.

He held his breath in amazement.

He was indeed in a great chamber. As his eyes grew accustomed to the dim light he could discern that there was a large, circular oak table surrounded by massive chairs, as if for a banquet. In each chair, slumped backwards or lying forward across the table, as if he were asleep, was a soldier in full, heavy, ancient armour of a kind Potter Thompson had never before seen. Each was a powerfully-built man.

Hardly daring to breathe he eased forward.

Each figure was as still as if he had been carved, like the painted stone effigies on a tomb or waxworks at a fair, yet they were not as still as dead men are, but as if they had been frozen in time.

As he got nearer he could begin to see each man's facial features, their beards, each distinct hair, scars on several faces, a broken nail. The eyes were closed, there was no movement or breath; each seemed covered with a patina of light dust.

In the centre, in a tall, high-backed chair, elaborately carved like a throne, sitting bolt upright, his hands together as in prayer, was a particularly imposing figure. By his regal presence and a superbly wrought golden coronet on his head of shoulder-length grey hair Potter Thompson knew he was in the presence of a mighty monarch, a great king.

Almost unconsciously his hand went to touch and finger the gold talisman which lay under his chemise. In spite of himself Potter Thompson was trembling, uncontrollably.

Each man had, by his side, a sword and an elaborately escutcheoned shield, both of such massive proportions that an average man would find them hard to lift, let alone wield in battle. These were great Knights indeed. Was this where his journey had led him, to a secret chamber deep under Richmond

Castle? There were twelve disciples of the monarch, awaiting their hour, the hour of need.

Had he, Potter Thompson, been chosen to awaken the mighty Prince?

It could not be. He would return to the outside world, to Richmond town, and bring wiser men than he to see this sight.

But would they believe him? What should he take as living proof of all that he had seen, so that his, a poor stone-mason's word, would be taken as the truth?

He peered through the gloom. Beyond the first table was another table, this time made of stone, a thick grey slab of rock, like an altar but of roughly hewn stone. On this slab lay a great sword in a thickly jewelled scabbard. Next to it, almost as thickly worked in gold filigree and jewels, was a large hunting horn.

Potter Thompson leaned across the table and picked up the heavy sword. It required both hands on the massive handle. He raised it a few inches above the table.

Immediately from the table behind him he heard a sound, a movement of limbs and armour, like men awakening. Potter Thompson let the sword drop. It crashed to the table, the sound clattering around the chamber.

There was complete silence. Nothing stirred, only his own stifled breathing. Potter Thompson looked round. Everything was quite still, frozen.

For a few seconds he didn't move. Then, on an impulse, he reached forward and picked up the hunting horn, and hardly aware of what he was doing brought it towards his lips.

Suddenly there was movement behind him—a creaking of chairs, a stirring of arms and armour, a groan. Then a voice, deep, powerful, full-throated:

'Is it time?'

Something snapped inside Potter Thompson. It was all too much. White with fear he flung the great horn down and fled. He stumbled towards the passageway, blind with panic and with fear, threw himself towards the daylight. As he fought his way through the cave a voice seemed to follow him, the words echoing through his skull, words he knew he would recollect over and over again for the rest of his lifelong days:

> 'Potter, Potter Thompson,
> If thou hadst either drawn
> The sword or blown the horn,
> Thou'd been the luckiest man
> that ever yet was born! '

Daylight dazzled him. Dizzily, he had to remember where he was and only just saved himself from falling headlong down the cliff by clinging to the roots of the ash tree. He stumbled down the slope onto the main path, back up the hill to Richmond town.

'Eh, Potter Thompson, lad, whativvers t'matter wi' thee', said Nancy Iveson coming down Bargate Hill, seeing a white faced, panting figure approach her. 'Tha' luiks as tha's seen a spirrit!'

'Ah've . . ., Ah've . . .,' stammered Potter Thompson. But no words would come out. He stood in front of Nancy Iveson, speechless.

And so it was with every other person he met that night.

'Potter Thompson has had one of his queer turns,' was the general verdict for weeks afterwards.

Back in the cottage where he tended for himself, Potter Thompson sat in the gathering twilight unable to either make supper or go to bed, reliving moment by moment everything that had happened since he had first noticed the cave.

Enraged with himself, he took a carving knife and stabbed it angrily into the table. But he took no rest that night, turning over and over in his bed until dawn when he rose, dressed, and made his way by the riverside path.

Sure enough there was the ash tree and the rabbit path, exactly as it had been yesterday evening. He struggled up the path, the earth and grass now wet with morning dew. There was the crevice, half hidden. He thrust himself towards it.

But his knuckles grazed themselves against solid rock. Angrily, frustrated, he kicked against the solid fissure which rose above him. He pressed it with his palms, as if it would open like a door, beat it with his fists, searched, above, below, to the side, frantically.

The sun was rising behind the town. It was hopeless. Who would believe him now?

> ' - Thou'd been the luckiest man
> That ever yet was born!'

Like a wounded animal, Potter Thompson gave a cry of pain.

The Drummer Boy

The workman kicked the stone.

'It's 'oller, tha' knows.'

His companion, a thin, undernourished youth who walked with a slight limp, crouched beside him. His master, a middle aged man with a grizzled and vast pot-belly surmounted by a thick leather belt, squatted on his enormous haunches and tapped the stone with a wooden mallet. The sound was unmistakable.

"Appen we s'll 'ave a look.'

He thrust the point of a trowel in between the stones, flaking away old mortar. Soon there was space to wedge the blade of a spade in to lever the loosened stone forward. They moved it from side to side, pulled it with their fingers and, after much puffing and grunting, managed to prize the heavy stone out, letting it thud out onto the ground.

Behind was blackness.

'God' s Blood,' said the older man, and he knelt forward, pushing his arm into the emptiness beyond.

They prized three more stones out leaving a gaping chasm in the wall. Behind was a mysterious space like a secret chamber.

'We s'll 'ave to tell t'Captain.'

So they made their way out of the tower and into the great courtyard of the Castle. A young subaltern was crossing the courtyard.

'An' beggin' yr pardon, sir,' said the workman respectfully. 'We've found an 'oile.'

'Anoil?' said the young officer, baffled. He had only recently joined the Regiment and hadn't mastered the subtleties of the local vernacular. But he followed the workman into the basement of the tower to view the newly revealed hole. He took a pebble and flung it into the blackness. It rattled onto a stone surface, echoing. It was clearly a deep space. He gasped in astonishment.

The Captain of the Guard was summoned and the experiment repeated. He hadn't seen anything like it before. So they summoned the Major. All three soldiers peered into the hole and agreed it was something quite extraordinary.

' Open it up! ' instructed the Major. The two workmen took up hammers and picks and, whilst the soldiers watched carefully, pulled out other stones till soon a perfect masonry archway, of fine dressed stone, was revealed. It led into what appeared to be a narrow passageway. It was no more than about five feet high and perhaps two feet wide, oval in shape but with a flattened bottom, too large to be a drain but not large enough to let a man pass easily.

'Well, and I'll be damned,' exclaimed the Major. 'What do you make of that?'

The others leaned across and gazed into the inky darkness and muttered.

'Like lookin' down into hell itself,' said the young workman, mournfully, 'though I can't smell any brimstone.'

A torch was sent for and one after the other they stared as far into the passage as the light of the spluttering flame would allow them.

The Captain and the Subaltern offered to go and look. Crouching, they made their way gingerly into the passage.

'There's steps,' said the Subaltern.

But they soon returned, their backs aching, their heads bruised, blinking in the daylight. Smoke from the torch filled the passage.

'Couldn't get further,' spluttered the Captain, coughing. 'Too much smoke.'

'How absolutely remarkable,' said the Major. 'Do you think it's some sort of escape route or hiding place?'

The thin workman spoke.

'If you please,' he began, 'there's a tale old folk in Richmond tell about a secret passage that runs from the Castle right through to Easby Abbey.'

'Old wives' talk,' said the Captain.

'No, wait a moment,' said the Major, reflectively. 'It's true, upon my word, that this ancient Castle has never been taken under seige. If the men who built this castle had made such a tunnel, it would be of enormous military advantage to get supplies into the Castle in time of seige, and perhaps even get a force out behind enemy lines. Simple—but brilliantly effective.'

'But it's over a mile, sir, between this Castle and Easby Abbey,' said the Captain.

'Ah you forget, sir, that the men of this Dale are miners—lead miners. "Groovers"—isn't that what they call them? Now they are well skilled in building underground tunnels. And wouldn't the Abbey provide just perfect cover? No doubt the secret would be well kept except in times of great trouble—for example the Scottish raids. Until this day, its secret had been lost.'

And he stood back on his heels in pride.

'We must investigate thoroughly. This could be of great importance to the defence of this Castle in these Jacobean times. But we must keep the matter a closely-guarded secret. There are people even in this town of Jacobite sympathies, and once the secret of this tunnel is discovered, its military value

'...there's a tale old folk in Richmond tell about a secret passage that runs from the castle to Easby Abbey...'

is lost—as our forefathers knew full well.'

And he smiled at his revelations. All were silent. The Captain expressed their fears.

' But is it safe, sir? I mean won' t there be danger? Suppose it fell in after years of disuse.'

'T'owd man's work. It'll be safe,' said the thin workman.

'Toad man? What do you mean?'

'T'owd man—that's a mining name, sir. The old lead miners. One or maybe two hundred years ago. They knew how to build tunnels like these. Taught by Germans, sir, so they say, metal workers from the Rhine. You see work like this, sir, in the Swaledale mines.'

The Major gave a low whistle of surprise. This was indeed a find. They must find out where it led straight away.

'We need a volunteer. Someone to go down there and find out where it leads.'

'It' ll have to be a small man—or a boy, ' suggested the Subaltern, uneasily, 'who doesn't have to bend down so far.'

'But how will we know where he is, underground?' asked the Major. 'We need to trace out the exact line of the tunnel, on the ground, so we know where it lies in case of any emergency. How we can achieve this I know not. '

'By noise, sir,' suggested the Subaltern, suddenly beginning to warm to the project.

'Noise?' asked the Major, incredulously.

'Yes, sir,' continued the Subaltern, now waxing enthusiastic. 'You know how noise travels through the ground—the sound of horses can be heard for miles along the ground. If someone can make a loud noise in the tunnel we'll hear it on the surface and that way be able to trace his steps as he walks from here to the Abbey, and furthermore, locate the exact place where it comes out. '

'Capital fellow!' exclaimed the Major, marking out the Subaltern as a young man worthy of early promotion. 'But who do we have who is small enough to walk through the tunnel and yet at the same time can make just such a noise?'

At that precise moment, walking across the courtyard, without a care in the world, came a little drummer-boy, a lad not fifteen years of age, in his full regimental uniform just back from parade. As he walked he beat the sid-edrum he was carrying slowly, idly, with his stick.

'Come here, Boy!' shouted the Major.

The boy leapt, terrified out of his wits, and froze to attention, wondering what army rule he had broken this time and what wrath was due to fall on his shoulders.

'HERE! '

The boy scampered across, his drum swaying. He stood to attention. He was a small lad, no more than five feet high with apple-red cheeks, a shock of flaxen-blond hair and, when he smiled, he smiled with a cheeky grin.

'Would you walk a mile for your Regiment, my Boy?'

The boy, bewildered, nodded.

'Can you make a loud noise, boy, with your drum?'

The boy nodded.

'Then MAKE it then!'

For answer the boy took up both his drumsticks and flicking his wrists as fast as he could, produced a terrifying, earsplitting din:

Ratatatatatatatatatatatatatatatatatatatatatat.

'Capital!' said the Major.

So they fixed him up, as the young workman suggested they should, with a cap with a tallow candle on it to light his way, as the old lead miners used to do. They told him to be a brave lad, and not to be afraid, and walk slowly and steadily, beating his drum as hard as he could all the way and they would follow him, walking on the ground just above him.

Ratatatatatatatatatat !

He began his walk. The others ran outside the Castle walls. Sure enough, they could hear the drumming, faint, yet clear, below them—*Ratatatatatatatat*. Sure enough, the sound began to move along the street, across the Market Place, under buildings, out the other side, through the town.

Passers-by carrying their shopping or going quietly about their daily business were astonished to see three soldiers cavorting drunkenly, pressing their ears to the ground, climbing over walls, vaulting over gates, into gardens, roaring with delight as they followed their hidden guide.

'He's here, ' cried the Major, leaping a wall like an excited schoolboy.

'Wait—now he's over here!' shouted the Captain as the ratatatat was clearly heard again as it passed right under a gentleman's rose bed. Then the sound passed underneath a house and they suffered paroxyms of anxiety until they heard the ratatatat again in the yard at the back.

Sure enough, the tunnel was heading directly down to the river and towards the ruined Abbey. The Major was beside himself with joy. What brilliant strategies he could plan, to surprise the enemy under cover of darkness, to slip supplies, and reinforcements in under their very noses. What a feat it would be!

Now the Drummer Boy was finding his way under the long meadows which lie beside the River Swale between Richmond Town and Easby Abbey, close by the footpath and parkland where, to this very day, unsuspecting tourists still stroll.

If anything, the drumming was now getting louder, as if the passage was rising close to the surface. They could hear every drum beat loud and clear. Somewhere, over there, among those gaunt and beautiful ruins just a hundred yards or so away, the Drummer Boy would emerge, his face breaking into that cheeky grin of triumph. The Major was beside himself with expectation.

Ratatatatatatatatatatatatatatat tatatatat tatatat tat tat

Tat.

Then silence. Why had he stopped, suddenly?

Silence.

They all stood still, held their breath, listened.

But no sound.

He had obviously stopped. After all, to drum away with such ferocity must cause the wrists to ache. He was resting. Soon he would start again.

Seconds became minutes. Nothing happened. They shuffled uneasily. Something was wrong, desperately wrong.

A feeling of panic gripped the Major. The Drummer Boy must be there, beneath the ground upon which they were standing. The Subaltern was sent back to the garrison to commandeer soldiers with spades and packages. They came, running. Soon, turves were lifted, earth piled in heaps and a broad trench dug several feet down. They worked in a frenzy but soon hit boulders and bedrock.

Where was he?

It was now late afternoon. The Boy could be lying there, injured. They had to get to him, quickly. They abandoned the digging, returned to the Castle. Candles were found, and a party sent down the passage.

In a few minutes they returned, their faces pale, bewildered.

'It ends—a chamber—and a wall . . .'

'Fools! ' said the Major, and pushed them aside. Taking a candle, he rushed into the passage, almost falling down the steps in his haste. This was the way the Drummer Boy had gone only an hour or so ago and he would still be there.

But at the bottom of the steps, sure enough, the passage ended. The Major held up his candle. He was standing in a deep, under- ground chamber, like a dungeon or tomb, carved from the rock where neither light nor fresh gust of air could penetrate. He walked slowly around the chamber, holding the candle close to every inch of wall, of roof, of floor for mark of doorway, passage or way to pass. But it was solid rock all round. He moved round and round, unable to believe his senses. He looked back up the steps. The walls were solid. Again and again he walked round.

At last his candle began to gutter. He returned, making his way slowly and heavily up the steps. When he emerged in the tower he found the others had already left, shocked and tired from their exertions. But they were not the one lost. And, after all, it had only been a Drummer Boy.

He stepped around the workmens' tools, abandoned where they lay. Tomorrow he would instruct them to rebuild the wall, to seal up this hellish passage for ever. He would have to make an official report of the incident. But no—the truth would not be believed by his superior officer. He would have to say that the tunnel had collapsed.

He looked across the courtyard to the lighted billet.

Above, the stars were just beginning to flicker their sharp points into the great dark blue dome of the sky.

Beyond the castle walls were the everyday sounds of the town, voices, wheels on cobbles, hooves, the clinking of glass.

But the Major was listening for the ratatatatatat of a drum and could hear only silence.

The White Doe

It was so still, so quiet. Only the river rippling past the stepping stones a few yards below the Abbey seemed noisy.

Swallows were skimming, swiftly, skilfully above the shallows, scooping up idling flies.

Eleanor made her way slowly forward towards the ruins. How noble! How perfect! These were the most richly picturesque ruins she had ever seen, in their magnificent setting of woods and hills.

She must sketch without delay. She must find the best perspective to capture their exquisite sadness, that sense of ivy-covered melancholia.

She walked up the gentle slope, towards the ruins. To the right was the graveyard, with its rows of mossy tombstones. Ahead, the Priory Church itself, according to the guidebooks still in use as the Parish Church of Bolton Abbey village, even while the chapels, dormitories, refectories and cloisters crumbled into decay.

She sat down on a stone in the middle of the ruins and took out her sketch-book and charcoal and began quickly, expertly, to sketch out the basic lines—the high, soaring arches, a shattered column. She would add some ivy over that one to give it a stronger, romantic feel. Later she would note the colours and, when at home with her easel, fill the picture with delicate greys and soft greens.

It was a warm, gentle afternoon and it was pleasant to sit and work in the late summer sun.

Within an hour most of the sketch had taken shape. In the centre was that tall Gothic arch, partially ruined, skeletal. She would put a tombstone in the foreground to give the picture depth. Grass and tendrils of ivy would give a feeling of the passage of time. She enjoyed adding such details, all sharply drawn from nature herself.

But something was missing. What the picture needed was life, movement. What should she put there? A monk perhaps?

Quickly she ghosted in an outline, a hooded figure. But it didn't work. It was the wrong shape—it looked grotesque. She rubbed it out. Something different was needed. She wondered what it should be.

Then it happened!

Through the archway it came—a small milk-white doe, slender and timorously shy. As she held her breath it came through the archway ahead

'Through the archway it came - a small, milk-white doe, slender and timorously shy.'

of her, its bright, sharp eye glancing up at her nervously. Eleanor stayed as still as stone. The doe leant forward to graze on a patch of grass growing between the flagstones. She watched it nibbling furtively, for several seconds. Then, almost as if it had heard a distant footfall, it turned round and vanished.

Eleanor laughed out with sheer delight. That was it—simply perfection. That would complete her picture.

But where had the white doe gone? She stood up and walked towards the arch where she had seen it. But there were only the ruins. No sign of the delicate creature.

'Would you tell me what you are doing here, please?'

Eleanor turned round.

The speaker was a man in clergyman's gaiters and frock-coat, a portly figure of perhaps forty.

'I'm—I'm sketching,' she said, suddenly aware of having done something wrong.

'Didn't you see the notice?' asked the clergyman.

'I'm sorry—what notice?' she replied.

'As you came into the Priory grounds. The Priory grounds are closed on Sundays. The Sabbath. Any other day you are most welcome. But the grounds are closed to visitors on the Lord' s Day. And sketching is expressly forbidden on the Sabbath. '

'Oh—oh I'm sorry,' she said as she folded up her sketchbook. 'I was travelling with my uncle from Harrogate and we're staying the night in the village. We specially broke our journey so that we could stay here.'

'I see. So you did see the notice?'

For answer she nodded gently.

'Let me see your sketch.'

She opened her book, guiltily, like a naughty schoolgirl. Perhaps he was going to tear it up as a punishment.

'Not bad. Not bad at all. You're very talented. You have captured the likeness quite exactly.'

'It's not complete,' she said. 'I have to add the White Doe— there'—and she pointed to the centre of the arch.

'The White Doe?' he said, looking up startled.

Almost as if on cue, the church bell, calling the congregation to Evensong, began to toll, its sharp, plangent sound echoing across the valley.

'Yes, it was here a few moments ago. I think it heard you coming. It seemed quite tame. Is it someone's pet or something?'

The clergyman was staring at her open-mouthed.

'My dear young lady—you have seen the White Doe of Rylstone. '

'The White Doe of Rylstone?'

'One of the saddest and most beautiful stories of the Craven Dales,' said the clergyman. 'And the White Doe is still seen, sometimes, usually by a woman or a young girl, just before or during Divine Service.'

'How extraordinary.'

'Look,' said the clergyman, 'it's far too long a story to tell you now. Come to the Rectory after dinner tonight. Bring your uncle with you—I'm sure he'd care to share a glass of port. And then I can tell you about the White Doe. The service begins in a few minutes. No doubt you will join us for Evensong.'

'That's very kind.'

Eleanor felt that she was obliged to join the service. So she took her sketchbook and box of charcoal into the church and sat in a pew towards the back. It was a small congregation, no more than twenty souls, mostly farmers and their wives in old fashioned country dress. Eleanor felt not a little conspicuous in her elegant coat and bonnet, more suited to the streets of Harrogate than a country church.

Small though the congregation was, they sang cheerfully and joined in the responses with a will, and only fidgeted a little during the parson's interminably long sermon.

Dinner was already being served as she made her way down the lane to the Inn. Her uncle was becoming anxious. She explained about her sketching at the Priory, The White Doe and the Parson.

Her uncle smiled.

'They've told me about him at the Inn. The Reverend William Carr. He's quite a character. He breeds cattle, has laid out many of the fine and picturesque walks through the woods that form the Duke of Devonshire's Estate here, and is a noted man of letters.'

So, after dinner, Eleanor and her uncle made their way down the lane to the Rectory. By now it was almost dark and the evening was decidedly chilly, so they were delighted to see a cheerful fire in the library of the Rectory. The Reverend Carr greeted them warmly.

'Mr James Bridgeton and Miss Eleanor Bridgeton of Berkshire,' he reflected. 'We get many distinguished visitors from all over England to Bolton Abbey. Tomorrow, for example, Mr William Wordsworth, the Lakeland Poet from Grasmere will be calling to see me.'

'How wonderful!' exclaimed Eleanor. 'I've read Mr Wordsworth's poems, *'The Lyrical Ballads'*, and consider them deeply affecting.'

'Quite so,' said Reverend Carr. 'I shall tell him about your meeting with the White Doe, you never know, it might excite his poetical fancy. Will you have some port?'

They sat down by the parson's fire, sipping the rich red wine.

'So—the White Doe,' began Reverend Carr. 'I take an unusual interest in these matters. Perhaps I don't have the busiest parish in Yorkshire, not like some of these new industrial towns springing up in the West Riding, so I serve the Lord in other ways. Did you know I was working on a dictionary of the Craven Dialect? Not quite Dr Johnson, of course'—he chuckled—'but mine own. Now I believe that the language of the common people in the Yorkshire Dales is as much a language as Welsh or Gaelic, and we must see it preserved, what with all the revolutions and changes in these turbulent times—new roads, canals, great flaring mills in every town which destroy our rural ways—sorry I digress. '

'Not at all,' said Mr Bridgeton.

'Perhaps you have read that marvellous set of volumes, *'Percy's Reliques of Ancient English Poetry'*, Bishop Percy's remarkable collection of ancient poems and ballads. '

'Indeed I have,' said Eleanor.

Reverend Carr rose, walked across to a bookcase and took down a well thumbed volume.

'Here,' he said, opening a book. *'The Rising of the North'*. This tells the story.

'It was really, I suppose, the story of a feud between two great families of Craven—the Cliffords and the Nortons.

'The Cliffords of Skipton, late Earls of Cumberland, one of the greatest families of all England, pillars of the State, once owned estates which extended from here to the Scottish border, and their descendants, the Cavendish family still own much of Wharfedale, including Bolton Priory.

'The Nortons, on the other hand, though rich and powerful in their own right, were nothing like as important or as influential as the Cliffords, but they did own quite a lot of land in Craven, most notably Rylstone, where the old Manor House was theirs, and hunting lands which extended right up to the moor.

'Hunting was the great bone of contention. Constantly Norton deer were being poached by Clifford men, and vice versa, most often vice versa, I suspect, but Clifford lands were very much more extensive. In fact, there were often pitched battles between the servants and retainers of the two families.

'It was also a question of politics and religion. In the time of Queen Elizabeth the Cliffords were loyal supporters of the Crown and of the Mother Church of England, whilst the Nortons were with the Old Church—they were Catholic, Papists, and those were intolerant times.

'But politics came into it in other ways too. The great families in the North ruled almost their own little kingdoms. London and the Queen were always a long way away. Did you know that Queen Elizabeth, never in her whole life, came further north than Lincolnshire? '

And he turned to Eleanor who shook her head.

'People in the North felt neglected, ignored. So the great families of the

North took matters in their own hands—men like the Percies of Northumberland, the Dacres and the Nevilles of Durham and North Riding, and the Nortons themselves. But they were mainly Catholic families, who, it was often felt, owed more allegiance to the Pope than to Good Queen Bess.

'Now, head of the Norton family at that time was one Richard Norton, known as 'Old' Norton because of his white hair and to distinguish him from his eight valiant sons. He was at one time Sheriff of Yorkshire and a member of the great Council of the North but, from all accounts something of a hothead, even in his old age.

'They had a house and estate at Norton Conyers, near Ripon, as well as the Manor House at Rylstone, but would come to Craven every summer for the hunting. They actually built a pleasure ground on the hillside, where they would practice archery, and a little stone tower, or summer house, that can be seen there on the hilltop above Rylstone. '

Reverend Carr drained his glass and placed it on a little table by his armchair.

Will you have some more port?' The others declined. He refilled his glass, and sank back into the chair.

'Now history came to intervene in the feud between Clifford and Norton in a quite extraordinary way. It did so in the form of that romantic figure, Mary Queen of Scots.'

When Eleanor heard the tragic, legendary name she sat upright on her chair.

'In 1598 Mary, a prisoner of her cousin Queen Elizabeth, was brought from Carlisle to Bolton Castle in Wensleydale where she was kept in the custody of Sir Francis Knollys. Many of the great Catholic nobles in the North came to Bolton to pay their respects to the Scottish Queen, and there seems little doubt that her presence in the Yorkshire Dales created a great deal of excitement and interest. I'm told you can even see a window-pane in a tower of the castle where she scratched her name with a diamond ring.

'She did, of course, try to escape, but was recaptured, some say on Leyburn Shawl, so the Queen decided to move her away from the area down to Gloucestershire.

'But it was too late. Already, throughout summer, at fairs and markets all over the North there was rumour and there was gossip. Rumours began to spread that the great Duke of Norfolk, himself of royal blood and ancient lineage, would marry Queen Mary and secure the succession to the throne of England, and, as many thought, the restoration of the Old Religion.

'Unfortunately for the Duke of Norfolk, Elizabeth got to know of the affair and the Duke was imprisoned in the Tower of London.

'The Northern Earls who had backed the idea of the Duke of Norfolk's marriage were thrust into a panic, fearful of their lives. They resolved to take matters into their own hands and raise the banner of open rebellion—the Rising of the North - which took place early in 1569. Richard Norton of Rylstone it was who raised the banner showing a great cross and the five wounds of Christ. And, gathering many of his sons and their men with him—Christopher, or 'Kit', Marmaduke, Frances, Thomas and others— joined forces with the Earl of Westmorland and the Earl of Northumberland at Brancepeth Castle in County Durham.

'The rebels then marched on Durham where they did terrible things, entering the ancient Cathedral, tearing up the Bible and destroying everything they felt was connected with the Protestant religion before saying the Catholic Mass in Latin in the Cathedral' s hallowed walls.

'Then they decided to march to York, forcing whoever they met on the way to join them at the point of a sword. But, by the time they got to Clifford Moor, not far from York, they realised that they would meet fierce resistance so they retreated. This time they travelled north back across County Durham where they laid a long seige to Barnard Castle, at that time defended by Sir George Bowes, a Protestant and a loyal supporter of the Queen.

'The Castle eventually fell, and the rebels were hoping to receive help from France and Spain via Hartlepools, on the coast, but that help never came. By this time the Earl of Sussex, Lord Hunsden, and a powerful army were setting out from York, to be followed by a still larger army lead by the Earl of Warwick, and hearing the news the rebels fled for their lives without an arrow or musket being fired. '

'But of course,' continued Revered Carr, 'the story doesn't end there. Many fled to the Scottish Borders into the hands of the terrible Reivers—the wild robber bands that once reigned supreme in those godless parts. Some, like Old Norton himself, and Francis Norton, managed to escape to the Continent and live in poverty and exile. Others were not so lucky. The ringleaders such as the Earl of Westmorland and the Earl of Northumberland were executed, whilst 'Kit' Norton and his uncle Thomas were hung, drawn and quartered in a horrible manner at Tyburn. Others, not so deeply implicated, were pardoned.

'But what was dreadful about the whole affair was that many of the common people, ordinary Dalesfolk doing no more than obeying instructions had, on direct orders of the Queen, to pay for the Rebellion with their lives. It was ordained that in each village where any man had taken part in the rebellion there would be a public hanging. Sir George Bowes himself, by all account a good, god-fearing and gentle man, had to carry out this harsh task, setting up a series of trials at which unfortunate men were to be determined guilty.

'There were executions in Threshfield and in Carlton, but strangely enough, as far as I can find out, not in Rylstone.'

Eleanor shuddered.

'It was a dreadful business done, I suspect, to ensure that never again in the Yorkshire Dales would there be open rebellion and insurrection. The Nortons, of course, were all either dead or exiled or disgraced and their estates taken from them. After a few years, and I think it surprised no-one, the Manor of Rylstone and the park and fell came into the possession of the Cliffords of Skipton as a reward, I suppose, for their loyalty to the Crown.

'So ended the 1569 Rising of the North.'

Reverend Carr sipped his wine.

'But what about the White Doe. The White Doe of Rylstone?' asked Eleanor, now puzzled to see the connection.

'Well that's the strange thing. After it was all over, a little white doe began to be seen at Bolton Priory, in the churchyard or among the ruins either just before or during Divine service. Old people used to say it came over the fellpath from Rylstone, and somehow embodied the spirit of the Nortons.'

'Was it a ghost?' she asked.

Reverend Carr shuffled impatiently on his seat. 'No,' he said. 'It wasn't a ghost. We don't have ghosts or any such nonsense at Bolton.'

'Then what was it? Is it real?'

He seemed to ignore the question.

'I like to think the White Doe was a real creature and that it was given by one of the Norton sons—perhaps Francis—to his sweetheart, and that after his banishment she would continue to come to this church to worship, her little white doe with her, as she prayed for his return.'

'And after her death it would still come on its own, knowing the way,' put in Eleanor. 'How enchanting!'

'Yes, that's a distinct possibility. And I suppose local people would continue to see it, in the same place and at the same time, centuries afterwards, outside the church awaiting her mistress.'

'How supremely beautiful!' cried Eleanor.

'You know,' said Reverend Carr, 'I have often discussed this tale with Dr Whittaker, the famous historian, and he has done me the honour of making reference to it in his *History of Craven*. When Mr Wordsworth calls tomorrow, I shall draw his attention to it, and to what you saw and what you suggest. After all, Dr Whittaker himself has suggested to me that the story would make the subject of a most beautiful and delicate poem. Let me read you what he says.'—and with that Reverend Carr rose and once again went to his bookcase, this time taking out a huge weighty tome. He rustled through the pages.

'Ah—just the place,' he said. 'Here. Let me read: "Had the milk-white doe performed her mysterious pilgrimage from Ettrick Forest to the precincts of Dryburgh or Melrose, the elegant and ingenious editor of the *Border Min-*

strelsy would have wrought it into a beautiful story. " '

'Who does he mean?' asked Mr Bridgeton innocently.

'Why—Sir Walter Scott, of course,' cried Eleanor impatiently. 'So do you think that Mr Wordsworth would accept the challenge?'

'Indeed he should,' replied Reverend Carr, 'and it is my firm belief that he should model his heroine on a someone as elegant and as charming as your good self, my dear young lady.

Eleanor flushed at the parson's words, not quite sure how she should take them.

'You do flatter me, sir,' she said.

' Hardly so. Surely you have to agree with me, Mr Bridgeton, that your niece would make a most agreeable heroine in any romantic novel or poem?'

Mr Bridgeton had no option but to agree.

Eleanor spent the rest of the evening telling the parson of her journey from Harrogate, where her parents had been for the season, to her Uncle James and Aunt Isabella' s house near Preston where Eleanor planned to spend part of September. They would take the coach again tomorrow from Bolton Bridge which made a useful connection with the Preston coach.

It was well past ten o'clock and quite dark by the time Eleanor and her uncle left the Vicarage to walk back along the lane to the inn. But before retiring Eleanor made her uncle promise that he would return with her the next morning to see the Priory once more.

* * * * *

Next day the weather, which had been fine for most of the month, broke, and heavy rain made the morning a miserable one. But Eleanor was nothing if not determined and, rain or no rain, she forced her uncle to accompany her to view the Priory ruins, and she pointed out the exact place where she had seen the White Doe. He was forced to admit that the setting was an unusually fine one and, even in the rain, the ruins extremely picturesque.

'I wonder if the men who built the Abbey here were aware of the beauty of this place,' pondered Eleanor.

'I'm sure they were,' her uncle replied.

Time was a little short and they had been warned that their coach, the *'True Briton'* , was often early, so they made their way along the lane back to the inn to collect their luggage and await it.

As they were walking along the lane, a wagonette came round the corner. Sitting in the back was a single gentleman. He was tall, lean, with a somewhat prominent nose, youngish, but already showing signs of premature balding. His clothes were well cut, if a little shabby, and a heavy cloak around his shoulders protected him from the rain. But his hair was wet and rain dripped incongruously from his long nose.

When he saw Eleanor and her uncle, he leant forward.

'Good day to yer, '—he had a strong, Cumberland accent. 'Could yer please tell me which is the home of Reverend William Carr—the Rectory that is. '

They told him where to turn off the main road down to the Priory, with the old Vicarage on the right hand side. He thanked them for their kindness and urged the driver forward.

'You know uncle,' said Eleanor, ' I'm quite sure that was Mr Wordsworth. '

'I'm sure it was,' replied her uncle.

'I should have spoken to him—about his verse. About *'Tintern Abbey'*, the most beautiful poem I have ever read. '

'That would have been a very vulgar and ungenteel thing to do. Do you think Mr Wordsworth has no better way to spend his time than to discourse with every young lady admirer? If he did so he would have no time to pen a single line. '

'I suppose you are quite right, uncle.'

They were soon at the inn, fussing about bags. The *'True Briton'* was indeed on time. Fortunately they had reserved seats inside. Soon they were swaying and rattling towards Skipton town and the horses heaved their way up Hambleton Banks along the turnpike road.

'Do you think Reverend Carr will remember?' she said suddenly to her uncle.

'Remember what?'

'To tell Mr Wordsworth about my White Doe and—and about his heroine?' she asked.

'Oh—I shouldn't think so,' he said. 'I'm sure they've far more important topics of conversation—matters of religion, of state, politics. They're not going to waste precious time gossiping about old tales and a phantom deer. '

'I suppose not,' she said, suddenly saddened.

She looked through the coach window across the little fields, each divided by pale limestone walls, the ash trees growing out of those walls, the scattered farmhouses. Even on such a grey, wet day, it was beautiful.

Then she remembered again the sharp, shy movements of her White Doe as it had appeared before her in that deserted cloister and her heart thrilled with the thought of it.

The Crock of Gold

In the cold grey before dawn, Emma lay in that half-conscious state between sleeping and waking. The warmth of her bed enveloped her like a cocoon. Yet the darkness invaded her, forced her into wakefulness.

So, it had been a dream after all. Yet it had been so extraordinarily vivid and real.

She knew the exact place it had happened—there, by the river-side. She knew the exact place having been there so many times in real life. She could see herself now, walking there, passing the great oak tree, and suddenly seeing the pot or urn filled with shiny gold. She had bent down to pick, touch the gold but as she had done so she found herself waking up.

So there she was in her narrow bed in the attic, with its low ceiling and garret-window now turning pale in the light.

She sat up. It had seemed so real, vivid and immediate.

Hadn't the Minister once told her that dreams were sometimes a sign from God, and could even be true?

Suddenly excited, she slipped out of the bedclothes and began to dress hurriedly. She found herself opening the door of her bedroom slowly, treading carefully not to wake anyone in the house, though the stairs creaked ominously.

She went into the kitchen, pulling a shawl around her shoulders and, taking care not to make a sound with the latch, opened the farmhouse door. She crossed the yard. One of the dogs barked, but no-one stirred. A cock crowed.

It was a cold, sharp morning of late summer, the grass of the fields wet with a heavy dew, whilst mist, thick and white, hung in the hollows. The first long rays of the sun were just beginning to light up the felltops. It was going to be a fine day.

She hurried over the stile, across the fields towards the river, her shoes soon soaked with the wet dew. Cows huddled together in a corner of the field with their flanks steaming.

She came to the riverside—the River Ure, swift, brown and deep, flowing through a narrow gorge just above the old ford.

There indeed was the tree—exactly as in her dream—a huge, ancient, mature oak, its vast branches twisted and sagged with age. She looked where, in her dream, the gold had lain.

With a stab of dismay she saw that no pot of gold was there—just worn soil and tree roots. She kicked the ground in her disappointment.

But where her foot had stabbed away the soil there was a faint curved stone. Curious, she took a stick and poked in the soil. A half-moon shape began to appear. As the soil was scraped away she saw it was indeed the neck of some kind of pot or vessel buried deep in the ground. More scraping revealed stones, earth and, underneath, black and round, some kind of small objects. She rubbed them against a stone. Sure enough they gleamed brightly.

So it was true! She had found, just as it had shown in the dream, a pot of gold buried under this tree. She found herself trembling with the excitement of it, afraid of what her discovery might mean. Almost beside herself with worry—the sun had now risen and she would be missed back at the farm—she had the presence of mind to cover up her handiwork, to scatter leaves, stones around to hide any trace of her activity until she had decided what to do about it.

Fortunately, the household was only just stirring when she returned. She hadn't been missed.

All that day, over her work, she thought about her dream and the gold. Her first thought was for the Minister, to go and tell him about the miracle. But what was the use? She was only a poor servant-girl; he would not understand. The Minister was too much like the old Squire, they'd take it all away from her. If God had wanted the Minister to find it, He would have let him find it. No. God had wanted her to find it.

As she beat the clothes in the dolly tub, as she scrubbed out the cheese press, as she baked oatcake she thought all the time about the crock of gold.

Hard physical work is an excellent antidote for insomnia, but Emma tossed and turned all night, her thoughts constantly returning to the oak tree, the urn, the coins.

Next day she rose again at dawn, but this time took a peat- spade with her down to the riverside. A few minutes fierce digging, breaking up the hard soil, prising back the tree roots which clung to it, revealed a broken pot, no more than eight inches high, the kind you might still find on any Dales farmhouse shelf, containing salt or goose-grease. But inside were scores of coins, some of differing sizes. She took one down to the river and scoured it clean in the river-sand. She could decipher letters but they appeared to be in a strange tongue.

Once again she covered her digging, concealed the spade in long grass. But she had under-estimated the time it would take her. When she returned, breakfast was being made and the fires not lit. She was evidently flustered and there was mud on her dress. Her stepfather would notice.

'We'er hast ta' bin?' he demanded, angrily.

'It were a nice mornin'. I went fer a walk.'

'Walk! Walk! Hast tha' nowt better ter do than laikin'. Ah'll mek thee walk!' and with that he aimed an angry blow in her direction which she had to dodge. He stormed out of the kitchen.

How she hated that man! Ever since he had first come to the house, her mother newly widowed. She remembered him, standing in the parlour, offering her poor distressed mother 'every help' on the farm she could no longer run herself, 'help' which was to lead to his gradual take-over of the running of the farm.

William Bland, 'Rantin' Bill' as he was known for his performances as a lay-preacher in local Methodist Chapels in his younger days, was a harsh man with a sharp-eyed peasant cunning. For him his neighbour Dick Fawcett's widow and daughter were but a means to an end—to create a viable farm out of two smallholdings.

She remembered how her mother, more and more dependent on her neighbour, simply let him manage her affairs and when he proposed marriage to her, a joining together of their two farms, she had been frightened to refuse. And after the marriage, the harsh words, the bullying ways. Her mother, unable to stand up to him, realised her mistake.

Once, Emma had come into the kitchen and found her mother sitting in a chair, in the dark, quietly sobbing.

Within a year she was dead, officially 'of a fever' but, as the neighbours said, of a broken heart.

And when Mrs Fawcett died, Emma was, in effect, disinherited, forced to be no more than a servant on her stepfather's farm, her own father's farmhouse locked up, neglected, as Bland ran the two farms as one. Indeed, Fawcetts' was the better land. Bland increased the stock, brought in hired men to help with haytime and shearing, forced Emma herself to work long hours, milking, cheesemaking, washing, cooking.

But what could she do? At twenty she was still too young to marry, nor could she simply leave the only place she could call home. She had an uncle who had emigrated to America some years ago, when the lead mines had fallen upon hard times, but she did not know if he were alive or dead.

The money she had found—whose was it? Intuitively she knew it was going to make a difference to her life, but she would have to keep her secret carefully.

All that day, too, as she worked, she thought about what she should do. At last she found she had decided. She went about her chores with a light heart, and that night, in her little attic room, fell into a deep and untroubled sleep.

The next daybreak she again rose and went down to the riverside, uncovered the pot, and took out a large handful of the coins, which she carefully concealed in a handkerchief in her sleeve. She took them back to her room, wrapped them in a piece of linen, and hid them under a loose floorboard beneath her bed.

Three times she repeated the journey, on separate mornings, until the pot had been emptied. And the next evening, when Bland was still out at the tavern, she took them out and by the light of her candle counted each small, round coin. There were 123 of them.

She had no idea what they were worth, but guessed that they represented a wealth beyond her wildest dreams.

Next Sunday, after Chapel, she collected a half dozen of the coins from the hiding place and, concealing them in her handkerchief, put on her coat and bonnet and walked up to the village.

The village of Carperby then, as now, straggled along the main road towards Askrigg. At the end of the village were a number of paupers' cottages, poor tumble-down dwellings where families lived who had fallen on hard times.

She knocked on the door of the Alderson's cottage where Lizzie Alderson, whose husband had been killed in the mines, lived with her four young children in conditions of real hardship.

"Ah've summat for yer, Lizzie,' announced Emma. Lizzie was sitting by a low peat fire, knitting. She looked up, expecting some small titbit for the children—a few eggs or a bit of gingerbread.

But Emma placed the six coins on the table.

'Tek 'em. They're gold. For thee 'nt bairns.'

Lizzie's eyes sparkled, unable to believe the miracle.

'Nay—I canna, Miss Emma,' she said. 'I durstna.'

'They're mine to give.' And she picked up the coins and placed them in Lizzie's trembling hands, folding Lizzie's fingers round the small, hard coins. There were tears in Lizzie's eyes.

'Now mek sure tha' spends it on them bairns,' Emma said.

She went back to the farm with a spring in her step. It was a wonderful feeling to bring hope and happiness. It was a feeling she had never experienced before—a feeling of power over other people's lives.

So she went back to her treasure hoard, took more coins and spent the rest of the afternoon calling at each cottage in turn, giving according to each person's need. Old Mother Foster, crippled and partly blind was given two coins, but Willy Taylor, who would just spend it on beer and bacca only got one. Families of young children, and there were several in the village, got most, especially if, like Lizzie Alderson, there was no wage-earner in the house.

And when she felt it was safe enough to take out the rest of her treasure, she found she had given away nearly forty of the precious coins. Eighty four remained. She would have to think carefully what she would do with these.

But hardly had she finished counting when she heard Bland coming back from the tavern. He had long given up his chapel going and most evenings stayed, drinking heavily until closing time. Tonight he had returned early and she was aware of voices. Somebody was with him.

Frantically, she returned the coins to their hiding place, concealed all traces, and made her way downstairs as if nothing untoward had occurred.

'Emma! Cum 'ere!' Bland's command was imperious.

Standing next to her stepfather in the little parlour was Squire Woodham, dressed in riding coat and boots. He was a heavily-built man, his face flushed with drink and the exertion of walking.

Emma had a horrified premonition of what was about to happen.

'What's up, Fayther?' she asked, the unaccustomed 'Fayther' almost sticking on her lips, only used to keep up appearances before strangers.

'Squire's summat t'ask thee,' he said.

She found herself trembling.

'Where did you get these, young woman?' asked Squire Woodham. He thrust three of the coins on the table in front of her.

She remained silent, horribly afraid. Someone had talked, probably in the Inn. It had been reported to Woodham.

'Answer!' demanded her stepfather.

'In't fields, ' said Emma, quietly, her voice hoarse from nervousness.

'Where?'

'In't fields. By t'river.' She glanced up at Woodham, the florid red face, long side-whiskers.

'You mean they were buried?' asked Woodham.

She nodded, afraid. But her mind was racing ahead. She must play for time. These two were after her money. Why should they, who had so much, have it?

'Do you know what these coins are?'

She shook her head.

'Spanish guineas. As far as I can make out sixteenth century. Pure gold. What you have found,' Woodham continued, 'was, if I mistake not, Spanish Armada gold perhaps buried here by an escaping Spanish sailor or privateer when the fleet was wrecked. No doubt he intended to return, but didn't live to retrieve his ill- gotten spoils.'

She continued to stare at him, wondering how to get herself away from them both.

'It's treasure trove, ' he said, finally. 'Do you know what treasure trove is?'

Emma shook her head.

'That means that any money found on your stepfather's land belongs to me, as Lord of the Manor. And I'm going to have every penny of it,' he said, raising and clenching his fist.

'Wh'er is it—rest of t'brass?' asked Bland, threateningly.

'Ah—Ah dunno . . .' she faltered.

'Who did you give it to? Who's got my money?' demanded Woodham.

'Ah've forgot. Ah don't right know . . .'

'Ah've a way to mek her spout . . .' began Bland, and he unbuckled his massive leather belt with its great brass buckle, and crashed it fiercely across the table. Emma leapt back in fear.

'There's no need to go so far,' interposed Woodham. Even he was shocked at the violence of the man. 'We'll get the information we need, and I promise you my man, when we do, you'll get a fair and good share, and one or two other matters we discussed besides. Lock her in her room and make sure she doesn't come out until I've a list of every person to whom she gave any money, and the whereabouts of every other single coin.'

Emma looked up at her stepfather in loathing. She knew full well the violence of his temper. There was no depth to which he would not stoop to get his own way. She could see the menace in his eyes.

It brought back to her memory that night two years ago, not long after her mother had died, when he had come back, fairly drunk and made crude and lascivious advances to her, his stepdaughter, fumbling at her skirt. She had kicked, bit the hand which held her shoulder, managed to break free, her dress torn, gone sobbing to her room, the chair wedged under the door to form a makeshift lock. All night she had huddled there, trembling with cold and fear, dreading his step on the stair.

But he had left her alone and next day, sober and sullen, avoided her for shame.

From that day to this she had kept him at a distance, each sharing a mutual antagonism, she a prisoner of her circumstance.

Intuitively, she sensed that things were coming to a head. This was the moment she had known for some time was coming. But, in spite of herself, she was trembling with fear.

'Get to thy room. And tha'll stay there and tha'll starve till tha does 'as Squire says. We s'll 'ave a full list of where ivvery penny on't is.'

She fled upstairs, trembling with fear, but with a wild light of excitement in her eyes. She knew exactly what she had to do.

Remembering what she had once been told about Scottish pedlars, she took needle and thread from her drawer and some scraps of material and, taking her old outdoor coat, began sewing, quickly and expertly, some hidden pockets along the inside of the coat like a second lining, placing the coins in them, dividing them up into sections so they wouldn't jingle. She worked far into the night until every coin was safely sewn inside—all 84 of them.

By this time the Squire had long gone and Bland, tired by drink, flopped into bed, so sure that she would remain in the house that he hadn't even bothered to lock the door.

She pulled on her boots, her coat, weighing heavy now, her bonnet, stuffing one or two tiny keepsakes into her pockets. Hardly daring to breathe she made her way downstairs, through the dark kitchen, feeling her way between chairs, unlatched the door.

Fortunately there was a soft, hazy moonlight, and she could easily see to make her way along the farmtrack to the road.

In Carperby she stopped at Lizzie Alderson's cottage, throwing stones at the window until, in her ragged nightdress, Lizzie appeared.

'Miss Emma—whativver's the matter?'

'Lizzie. The Squire's after me brass. Hide the brass from t' Squire. Save it for t' bairns'.

'Ah will lass. '

And Emma reeled off a list of the most deserving cases to warn that the Squire would be seeking to rob them of what she had given them. Lizzie promised on the Holy Bible she would.

Emma made her way along the long dark road, running and walking as she could. She was a strong, fit lass but the heavy coat and bonnet slowed her progress. How long would it be before her stepfather found she had gone and raised the alarm?

She would have to get as far as she could before dawn, and then either take to the fields or hide. But it could be dangerous if anyone suspected that she had so much money on her.

After about an hour and a half she reached the town of Askrigg. But dawn was not far away. The first cock crowed, there was light to the east behind her. She hurried through the little town, past the market place, the church, the clockmakers' cottage.

Daylight was coming. She heard hooves behind her and turned, afraid. But it was a carrier, leaving at daybreak to get to Kendal market.

'Dos't tha' want ta ride, maid?' asked the carrier, a pleasant- faced fellow. There was nothing else she could do.

She accepted his hand up to the front of the heavily-laden waggon and they rode together along the winding road up the Dale.

'Ah'm goin' ter Settle,' she said. 'To see my aunty.'

'Tha's left early,' he said.

'It's a long way.'

She knew he didn't believe her but he was a quiet dignified man, of early middle years, with a shock of white hair above his weatherbeaten face. As he rose he pulled a battered hat to the back of his head. She learned that he made this journey once a week and that he had a wife and two grown-up sons. She avoided saying too much about herself.

By now it was daylight, a grey, cold morning with an autumnal nip in the air. Ahead was the town of Hawes, its little church tower dwarfed by the size of the massive fells all around.

They swung off the back road, down towards the river.

'Ah'm stoppin' fer a bite o' breakfast, ' said the carrier. 'Will tha' keep an eye ont' cart fer me?'

Outside the tavern Emma waited in the cold whilst the carrier went inside for some bread and cheese and a tankard of ale. When he came out he had a piece of bread and chunk of thick, white Wensleydale cheese in his hand for her.

'Tha' looks as if tha' s not had owt to eat for a while, ' he said. She took the bread gratefully and ate, nibbling the cheese. He looked up at her, holding the horses reins as he did so.

'Summat's up wi' thee, lass,' he said finally. 'It's not for me to enquire of another body's trouble, but if ah can help thee, ah will.

She looked at him, unsure if she could trust him. But his eyes were gentle.

'Ah've run off,' she said finally. 'Me stepfather.He's bad to me.I don't want him to find me.'

'Will he cum after thee?' he asked.

'He might.'

'Where art tha' off to?'

'Me Aunty' s — in Settle . ' She was aware of herself lying . She had no aunt in Settle. But she didn't want him to know she had nowhere to go.

'Appen, he'll know where tha' went and come after thee,' he concluded. 'Keep off the road in daytime. Travel at night. There's 'undreds do it, so's not to be seen.'

They trundled off through the little town. Shopkeepers were just opening up, the baker had a huge tray of loaves to deliver. He ignored the travellers.

They came to the cross-roads just above the town. The Settle road was to the left, the Kendal road branched off right.

'Sithee, lass,' said the carrier. 'Now don't tek the coach-road, t' turnpike. Tek the old road, left, just past the tollbooth. It'll climb up Dodd Fell, there's not many uses that way, except on foot, and he's less likely to catch thee there.

'Now just up t' road, on t' left, tha'll find an old barn. It belongs to Neddy Capstick and he'll none trouble thee. Settle thy self there fer t' day and travel on thy way at night. Nobody'll trouble thee then. '

It seemed to her excellent advice, so she said farewell to her kind companion and set off up the hill.

At the tollbooth, the turnpike keeper saw her pass.

'Art goin' far?' he asked.

Wouldn't she be recognised if her stepfather asked him? Emma thought for a moment.

'Just to visit me grandma',' she said.

'Is it far?' he asked.

'She lives in a farm up ont' Settle road,' she said.

'Up Widdale? Or Newby?' he asked.

'That way,' she said. They were places she had never heard of.

'What do they call her?'

Emma panicked. Her story was wearing thin. One lie always led to another.

'Metcalfe,' she said, trusting there'd be plenty of Metcalfes on the Settle road.

'Never heard on 'em,' said the tollkeeper.

But he let her pass, obviously puzzled.

Soon after a horseman came riding by. Instinctively she flattencd herself against the wall, but he passed her without a word.

On the left, the track that the carrier had described branched off. It was a stony way, once the main road, but since the new road had been built a few years ago, disused except for the occasional drover with cattle, sheep or even geese.

And sure enough, on the left was the barn, an old decrepit structure. She went inside. There were empty cattle-bays and above, a loft storing hay. She climbed the ladder-stair, and looked round for a comfortable place in the hay to rest.

A sound disturbed her. It must have been a rat. In the gloom she could see what appeared to be a bundle of rags.

At that moment the bundle of rags sat up, sprang to its feet and within seconds a knife was pressed to her throat. Her attempted scream was stifled as a hand was pressed across her mouth. She struggled, thrusting her assailant backwards, for she was a strong girl, and for a few seconds they rolled on the loft floor, she pressing the knife away from herself with all her strength, and terror in her eyes.

She found herself staring into the face of a youth, scarcely her own age. As he realised she was a girl his grip relaxed and she sprang free.

'Do anything to me, an' I'll scratch thy eyes out,' she flashed, facing him, ready to defend life and honour to her last drop of blood.

But he only laughed.

'Nay—nay lass. Ah thowt thee were cum ter tek me.'

She looked him up and down. He was a slight, even slender youth, in truth no real match for Emma who was a big-boned lass. He was wearing ill-fitting torn clothes which she soon recognised as being the remnants of a soldier's uniform.

He threw the knife down and held out his hand to her.

He was dirty, dishevelled and clearly had been living rough for some time. A fine, downy beard covered his cheeks.

'Who art thi'?' she asked, suspicious.

He sat down on a bale of straw. He began to tell her his story. His name was

'Ahead was the town of Hawes, its little church-tower dwarfed by the size of the massive fells all around.'

Jim Horner, he had been born on a Dales farm and worked as a farmhand and in the Burtersett quarries. Then, one day, the Recruiting Sergeant had come to Hawes and had invited him into the pub. After being bought a pint or two of the *White Hart's* best ale, the Sergeant had invited him to accept the King's Shilling, and having listened to the brave words and promise of travel to far off lands, he had done so. Before he knew what had happened he was saying farewell to his tearful mother and was being marched off to barracks.

He had hated army life, the harsh discipline, the drill. And when he had discovered that the Regiment were going to France to fight Boney's men, he had thought of himself lying dead in a foreign land and had run away, deserted. He had travelled across England for three weeks, fearful of getting caught to face a firing squad, stealing food to live. He had come back home to the Yorkshire Dales but was terrified to show his face in case they found him.

She told him that she, too, was running away, from a cruel stepfather who would chase her and beat her. She did not tell him of the money. That could wait. But they agreed to travel together as long as he would promise her there would be no 'wickedness'.

So they improvised rough beds in the straw and he shared with her a loaf he had stolen.

And they slept most of the rest of that day.

By late aftemoon, they decided to continue their journey, following the long, stony track up the fellside. It was a mild, cloudy evening, the lights of the scattered farms below them and Hawes behind them in the distance. It was a lonely way but easy to follow. Gradually the light drained away.

They walked on, talking about their experiences. He knew the carrier, Tom Ingram, who had given her the lift. He spoke of people he knew in the little town. He would have liked to have had his own farm one day but now it would never be. She told him about her real father, his death after being gored by a bull, her mother's sorrow at the funeral, the way 'Ranter' Bland had gradually come to control and dominate her. As she was talking she realised that she had never opened her heart to anyone like this before, and him a perfect stranger too.

Where a little stream glistened its way across the track, they stopped and drank gratefully from the flowing water. By now the cloud had cleared a little and a diffused moonlight lit the old road ahead. In the distance they could see the awesome shape of the mountains—the massive bulk of Ingleborough ahead. Emma had never before in her life been so far from home and the sight of the hill's silhouette frightened her. They had reached the summit of the track over Cam Fell, where it joins the stony Roman Road from Wensleydale, and began the descent into Ribblesdale.

At a cross-roads they puzzled the way. Jim thought it was to the right, but Emma noticed a milestone upon which was carved a crude hand and the name of the town - SETTLE. Being able to read from her time at the village school, she was able to decipher the letters, partially by touch and partially by sight in the half-light.

The way was indeed left and they plunged down the hillside, over Ling Gill Bridge and along the shoulder of the hillside into Ribblesdale.

By now they were footsore and, seeing another barn close to the track, made their way to it. This time they found there were cattle in the byre, but once again made their way to the hayloft and within a few minutes were asleep, hardly aware of the fact that they were pressing against each other for warmth.

The next thing Emma knew was the door of the barn being flung open and an elderly woman carrying a backcan on her back and a pail in her hand stumbled in. Jim woke with a start and instinctively she signalled to silence him. They watched as the woman took a stool, sat herself down heavily and, with a steady pumping motion of her hands, began to milk each cow. Just a few feet from her head the two of them lay, hardly daring to breathe. The rich, steaming jets of milk splashed into the pail.

After what seemed to be an age, the woman moved to the next cow and began the process again, only pausing to pour the milk carefully into the can. As the milking went on, Emma was aware of a desperate itching in her foot, but she dare not stir or move.

At last, all six cows were milked, the milk poured into the can, the door opened and the cows let out into the field. The woman, slipping the heavy can onto her shoulders, the weight causing her to stoop, made her way slowly across the field.

Danger had passed but it no longer seemed safe to stay. So they quickly made their way over the field, back along the old road.

'We must get ter Settle,' said Emma, now determined upon a plan. Suddenly bold, in spite of sore feet, she urged Jim to press ahead, the way passing farms, down to Horton-in-Ribblesdale.

They followed the main road down the valley. If anyone came, they would quickly take shelter before being seen, hiding behind a wall until the person had passed.

Everyone in Horton was seeing to their own affairs, too busy to notice a tired young woman and a ragged soldier. They followed the road to Stainforth, to Langcliffe.

It was Market Day in Settle. By now it was a hot afternoon and Emma felt absurdly hot in her bonnet and heavy coat. But it could not be taken off, just yet.

'Ah've ter meet someone,' she said. 'Ah want ter get summat sorted. Hide in yon wood.'

And she left him in a little copse, concealed in brushwood and ferns. Then she went to the river, washed her hands and face, smoothed her hair.

Boldly, she walked into Settle town. The market-stalls were bustling with farmers, farmers' wives and wives of millworkers from the textile mills now flourishing in the valley.

She saw the building she wanted, to the left of the Square. The Craven Bank.

Inside it was crowded with farmers, all handling their weekly bills and accounts. She saw sovereigns being handed over the counter.

She waited her turn and, when it came, asked to speak particularly to the Chief Clerk.

'Have you an appointment, Miss?' asked the clerk at the desk.

She explained she hadn't but it was particularly urgent.

The clerk went to the back and whispered with his superior. Emma was told to wait.

She waited for almost half an hour then was ushered into a small room where a thin, middle-aged man, almost completely bald and wearing a pince-nez was sitting behind a large, leather-covered desk.

'Can I help you, young lady?' asked the Chief Clerk.

'Ave sum brass to put int' bank,' she said.

It was something the Chief Clerk of the Craven Bank was to remember for the rest of his life, how a young woman, in a creased and dishevelled coat had come into his office and without further ado had started tearing at her coat, and one by one filling the top of his desk with a collection of antique Spanish gold guineas.

At first he was thrown into confusion. This was not coinage of the realm. But this young woman was not to be deterred by such niceties.

'It's brass and worth a lot. Tha can sell it for me. And put it in my name. '

Was she a thief or vagabond? But she looked respectable enough. Where had she got such fabulous wealth?

'It was me Mother's. And she got it off me grandfer'. And she's died and told me to bring it to you . . .'

Was it true? Perhaps she was lying.

But business was business. And when the Clerk had counted up 84 golden Spanish guineas he whistled to himself in amazement.

'What's your name young lady?'

'Emma'—she paused. It was just possible that even here Bland could trace her. Or Squire Woodham. 'Emma Metcalfe.'

She signed her new name with an elegant flourish, even remembering to add the 'e'.

Emma did more business that afternoon. She was to receive five sovereigns on account, and when the guineas were sold at a reputable outlet which Mr Bailey the Chief Clerk would arrange, her account would be credited. And yes, he would arrange for her to meet a colleague who had a suitable property to rent, a fine small-holding with some forty acres of prime Ribblesdale land and looking for a suitable tenant.

She took her sovereigns and bought a shirt, trousers, boots, a jacket, and some food.

When she got back to the wood, she found Jim looking despondent.

'Ah thowt tha'd left me . . .'

His soldier' clothes were buried in the wood. They walked back into town. Separate rooms in the town's best inn were booked. Whiskers were shaved, hair cut.

Over a dinner of veal and ham pie and excellent ale, Emma laid down her terms.

'We' ll do everything proper and respectable like. Tha' d better be Jim Johnson from now on. Tha' can come with me tomorrow and 'ave a look at the farm. If ah like it, tha' can help me with the stock and the work, as the hired man, and we'll see how it all shapes out.'

Nothing more than that. No use being sentimental about such matters. But now he was clean and tidy he was a neat, dapper young fellow and a lass could do worse . . .

After all, that hadn't been in the dream, now had it?

Hunting the Barguest

'A Barguest,' said the grey-haired gentleman sitting in the comer of the little Dales pub, 'is a curious phenomenon. You find versions of this legendary beast popping up in the folklore of many countries throughout Western Europe.

'It's usually described as a great dog, a spectre-hound. In Germany he's referred to as "Wüthrich", a name linked to Woden, I presume. In the Isle of Man he turns up as The Mauthe Dog, meaning the Death Dog. In Alsace Lorraine they call him "Dorf Thoir Ghost" whilst in Derbyshire he's "Hell Dog."

'Even in Yorkshire he's got different names. Leeds people warn their children about "Padfoot", whilst only down the road in Skipton he's known as "Trash" or "Guy Trash".

'I've never had the misfortune to see a Barguest myself, but I'm told he's a great black dog with one big eye in the middle of his forehead who comes out of the sea and haunts narrow lanes, and woe betide you if you meet him.

'I've absolutely no doubt that he's largely the result of a too frequent indulgence of this fine stuff here, ' and he sipped his glass of old Yorkshire ale.

He looked round the room. It was a cold, January evening with a coal fire roaring in the grate. There were half a dozen other people in the room, mainly farming men.

'I don't believe a word of it,' he continued.

'Ah'm sorry to contradict thee, Dr Dixon, ' said a voice . ' But ' ees about.'

'Who's about?' asked the old scholar, looking quizzically across his beer glass.

' t' Barguest, ' said the voice . It was Daniel Cooper who spoke, an old farmer from Linton.

'Why—has tha' seen one?' said Dr Dixon lapsing into dialect.

'Appen 'ah seen an odd un now and then. And Billy Blakey, he's seen one sure enough. He were comin' back fer a clock dressin' a Girston, an he met 'un int' loin. An' Billy were a Methodi', a Chapel Man, and didn't sup too much, least not more than were good fer ' im. '

'Aye, but when dids' t tha' last see one, Daniel? ' asked Dr Dixon.

'It were a bit back, that I admit,' said Daniel. 'But I remember it.'

'What did it look like?'

"Appen, as tha' described it, big wi' a girt 'ead.'

'An 'appen tha'd a pint or two at the time,' said Dicky Wilson.

'That a didna',' retorted Daniel angrily.

'Poor old Daniel,' said Dr Dixon. 'Nobody believes you.'

'All right, all right. Will ta cum wi' me, toneet, ter Troller's Gill, an 'appen see un fer thi' sen?'

'It's late.'

'Will ta?'

'It's too late, Daniel ol' lad. Time you were in bed,' said Dr Dixon.

'I'm game,' said Jimmy Lister, a young man who had been listening to the conversation with interest.

'Me too,' said Jack Lambert, his friend.

'Aye—go on, aye, ah'll cum wi ye,' said Dicky Wilson.

'Tha'll not be backin' down now, will tha Dr Dixon?' said Daniel. 'It's a fine neet.'

'Plenty o'moonlight. Almost as bright as day out the'er,' said Jack. He wiped the steam away from the pub window. Outside was a clear, frosty night, the moonlight soft, making the low Wharfedale hills gleam as if they had been silvered. Every star was as sharp as a pin-point in the great dome of the sky.

'It's too far to walk,' protested Dr Dixon, now feeling distinctly uncomfortable.

'Dicky's got 'is oss 'n trap outside. We'll all on us get in,' said Jimmy.

'No. I really don't . . .'

But they were all looking at him. He was about to lose face. There was no getting away from this one. With a sudden surge of bravado Dr Dixon drained his glass and rose to his feet.

'All right then. Let's go and meet the Barguest.'

Outside the pub, the raw cold greeted them. Dicky Wilson's horse and trap were there as promised. They clambered in. Dicky untethered the horse and they set off along the lane towards Burnsall at a steady trot.

The soft moonlight reflected from the pale limestone walls to give a ghostly effect. It was indeed almost as bright as daylight to which the frost added a distinctive sparkle. But everywhere the shadows were long, deep and mysterious.

As they trotted along, Dr Henry Dixon, scholar, historian, wit, reflected on the strange impulse which had led to him accepting this curious challenge. What was he doing here, a man in his mid- sixties, an authority on Dales life and lore, out in a dog-cart with a bunch of inebriated villagers chasing phantoms at midnight? What on earth had possessed him to enter this mad escapade?

But, notwithstanding the cold, it was a superb night, an occasion to be cherished. Would this not make a suitable entry, with adequate, elegant embroideries, in one of his *Notes and Queries* in a future *Hone's Table Talk*?

'It's a bonny neet for Barguest 'untin,' said Daniel Cooper.

'That it is, Dan. 'Appen tha' ll see ' alf a dozen, ' chipped in Jimmy Lister.

'And flying pigs and ladies on broomsticks sailing by,' added Dr Dixon.

As they rattled through Burnsall, the last revellers were being turned out of the *Red Lion*, staggering drunkenly across the fore- court.

' Out ot t' rooad,' cried Dicky Wilson, urging the horse forward. They crossed the river by Burnsall Bridge. The broad curve of the Wharfe shimmered quicksilver from the moon's long reflection. They followed the lane towards Appletreewick. At the steep hill through the village the pony struggled to a halt, and they had to dismount and walk alongside. The brisk walk warmed them.

Maybe the joke's gone on long enough, thought Dr Dixon. But the others were clearly enjoying every minute of it and what better night for a midnight walk? At the top of the hill they stumbled back into the trap and jogged past the cross roads towards Skyreholme, soon turning left towards Parcival Hall.

At last they came to the little ford below Troller's Gill.

'It's nobbut ten minutes' walk from 'ere,' said Dicky, tying the pony to an ash tree by the lane side.

'Ah think ah'll stay and look after t' 'oss,' announced Daniel.

'I thought tha' were leading t' way,' said Dr Dixon.

'Ah, but at my age, ah'm gettin' a bit past midnight trampin',' replied Daniel. 'Ah'll bide 'ere till ye get back.'

So the four of them set off—Jack and Jimmy, Dicky Wilson and Dr Dixon.

They followed the path by the stream, past a barn, over a stile, the path winding up the hillside a little, along the side of the valley.

The moonlight made the going easy. Detail was surprisingly clear. But it also gave the little valley a strange, dreamlike quality, as if nothing were quite real. An owl, white and dusky, hooted and flapped past.

They were entering a narrow, rocky valley. At either side rose steep limestone crags, which gleamed eerily in the soft light, their overhangs forming deep shades. You could see where the little caves were in the valley sides—wells of inky blackness. The stream in the valley bottom flashed its silver. It was an impressive sight even to those, like Dr Dixon's companions, not normally of poetical disposition.

They came to the point where the valley divides—the left leading via a broad miners' path into a shallow valley filled with old lead-mine workings, the way on the right into Troller's Gill itself.

Jack was fumbling in the pockets of his immense poacher's jacket.

'Appen as it's time fer a lile refreshment,' he said, producing a bottle of brandy from deep within a pocket. He unscrewed the top and took a deep swig .

' Dicky—Jimmy—Dr Dixon .' He offered the bottle around.

'No thanks,' said Dr Dixon.

But the others had already sat down on a limestone boulder and were passing the bottle around, oblivious to anything but the rich warmth of the brandy as it lit their insides.

'I'll walk on a short way,' said Dr Dixon. There was something about this place which, after all, fascinated him.

He clutched his silver-topped walking cane and turned towards the mouth of Troller's Gill, a few dozen yards ahead. It is a deep cleft in the limestone, no more than two or three yards wide, and several deep, through which a shallow beck trickles over the stones.

It was pitch black, black as a cave in there, and Dr Dixon had to nerve himself forward. Holding his stick, he plunged into the darkness, feeling his way along, his feet stumbling over the boulders and rough stones. He'd been before often enough, though never in darkness, and could guide himself by memory and by instinct.

After a few yards of feeling and scrambling, he found himself once more in moonlight as the gill opened out to a broader gorge.

It was like standing in a strange and mysterious amphitheatre. The effect of the moonlight was to heighten and intensify everything. The edge of the ravine looked immense, the little yew trees growing from high crevices like ragged pines. The crags seemed to adopt strangely carved shapes, towering above, menacing. The stream, fast-flowing, glistened and gleamed. Anything could happen in a place like this.

He walked forward, hesitant. The gill curved round slightly, narrowing between even steeper walls of rock, vanishing into more blackness where the moonlight could not penetrate.

When it came it did not seem all that surprising. It was huge and black, like a wolf but much, much larger, its single eye, as big as a saucer, burning from its forehead, its thick black fur long and matted. It seemed to emerge from the very blackness of the gill ahead and lope towards him, striding heavily past him, its body-weight flopping, yet where its large clawed feet fell no stone was disturbed, no stone rattled.

It loped past within inches of him and as it passed, even through the cold of the night, he felt an additional chill, an icy blast to his cheek. He would have cried out in fear and terror but his voice was silenced to a gasping croak as he turned to watch it make its heavy way down the gill below him, its dark wolf tail vanishing into the blackness below.

He stood there transfixed with fear for several seconds. It was like some terrible nightmare, unreal yet horrifying in its vividness. He winced, to make

'...towards the mouth of Trollers Gill, a deep cleft in the limestone, no more than two or three yards and several yards deep...'

sure he was quite awake, and he fingered the top of his silver cane, the familiar shape and engraved decoration. It was real. He trembled with fear.

He must pull himself together. What had he seen? Was it indeed the legendary Barguest, or had the whole thing been a figment of an elderly man's fevered imagination, the result of too many years spent with old books and manuscripts in libraries and smoke-filled rooms until something within the deepest recesses of his mind, like a great black beast of the night, had suddenly broken free and loped down the ravine past him.

That was it. That was what it had been.

But as he recalled the intense vividness of that burning, blazing eye, he knew that could not be.

What would they all say? What would people think? He, Dr Henry Dixon, man of letters and learning, one time inhabitant of Craven, now of Lausanne in Switzerland, returning for a short holiday in Yorkshire, having seen a Barguest. Who would believe such balderdash? He would be the laughing stock of half of Europe. That simply would not do. It wouldn't do at all.

Far better to pretend the whole thing had never happened. His reputation must be protected at all costs.

So even though he was paler than the pale moonlight, and trembling like an ash leaf in November, Dr Henry Dixon made a faltering and stumbling way back down the narrow neck of the gill, into the blackness in the very steps of the fiercesome Barguest itself.

The others were still sitting there. After all, he'd only been away a matter of a few minutes. Even if the Barguest had rushed right past them, they'd have scarced looked up from their drinking, not seeing it.

'We thought t' Barguest had aten thee,' said Jimmy Lambert, delighted at the jest.

'We've saved thee a sup,' said Jack, holding out the brandy bottle, now only half full, towards the stumbling figure.

'Thanks,' said Dr Dixon, seizing the bottle and, to everyone's surprise, taking a deep and extended draught.

Jack looked at the declining level of brandy in the bottle with further surprise.

'Silly bloody nonsense,' said Dr Dixon. 'Bloody nonsense.' And he took another shot of brandy. The others looked at each other in amazement. They were not used to such language from Dr Dixon, Doctor of Divinity.

'Time we were away,' he said, and began to stride determinedly along the path to the pony and trap. The others, because they were now beginning to freeze with cold, ran after the striding figure of the scholar like schoolboys discovered in some naughty prank.

When they got back to the pony and trap they found Daniel Cooper asleep under a rug he'd found in the bottom of the trap. They prodded him awake.

'Nah then, Dr Dixon,' he growled. 'Didst tha see t'Barguest? Hast tha' brought 'im back wi' yer?'

Nay, ah've brought nobbut three drunks ah found ont' way,' said Dr Dixon.

They all scrambled on board and Dicky took the reins, turning the horse round and setting off at a quick trot back towards Linton.

It proved a slow journey home, well past midnight as it was and everyone, with the exception of Daniel Cooper, a good deal drunker than when they had started out from the inn. Their drunkenness had gone well beyond the superficial stages of merriment to a point of deep melancholia where, through a rich alcoholic haze, only added to by the moonlight, they saw to the very heart of things, to the essential sadness of the world and its evil ways and the need for everlasting, warm friendship.

Sad were the songs sung or, more accurately, howled as the party made its slow way back along the lanes to Linton. Luckily only the sheep in the fields were there to raise their heads to the sound of off-key voices and clopping of hooves.

As the moonlit stone roofs of Linton came into view they all agreed that Barguest or no Barguest it had been one of the best nights out ever. The empty brandy bottle rolled across the floor of Dicky Wilson's trap.

It had already been agreed that Dr Dixon would be spending the night with his old friend Daniel Cooper before returning next day to his lodgings in Skipton.

Before they retired, the two friends sat down for a few moments by the dying embers of Daniel's kitchen fire.

'So tha' nivver saw t' Barguest?' asked Daniel.

For answer, Dr Dixon permitted himself only the most enigmatic of smiles.

Batty Moss Wife

The drumming of rain on a wood and tarpaulin roof - repetitive. She looked through the window, watching the water stream down. She looked across the rows of huts towards the scaffolding on the great, half-finished viaduct. Beyond the viaduct the lower slopes of Whernside, grey and uninviting, vanished into low and heavy cloud.

It seemed to have been raining for days. There was water everywhere, great pools in the walkways between the huts, streams breaking their banks but, in spite of the weather, work was still going on. She could hear the chuff-chuffing of the little steam locomotive on the tramway on its way up the great embankment side.

She lay on the bed, pulling a single grey blanket around herself. She was feeling the cold and the damp. The oil stove gave little or no heat in these grim days of late winter. It was the beginning of April, but still as bleak and as cold as December up here. How she hated the place!

She was increasingly uncomfortable as the weeks passed. It wouldn't be long now before her baby was born but the weight was heavy and she was finding it difficult to move around or to lie comfortably. The thought of the birth frightened her. There was a small hospital here and she would go there when her time came - many children had been born in the camp and seemed healthy enough. But this was no place to bring up a child.

How had it happened? How had she come to be in this dreadful place she so wished to get away from?

As she huddled under the blanket the events of the last year raced through her mind.

It had started innocently enough. Alfred had seemed a nice lad, bit of a rough diamond perhaps, but warm hearted in his way and a girl needed to have a nice lad to walk out with on Sundays.

She'd known him since their schooldays. She'd looked down on him then, one of the rough kids whose dad worked in the Gunnerside Gill lead mines whilst she, Betty Thwaite, came from a good Swaledale farming background.

But after he left school and became a miner himself, he'd grown into a handsome, well-made lad, even a bit of a dandy in his way with a fine black moustache and a shock of dark hair. And he was earning good money.

'Wilt tha' cum out wi' me?' he'd asked her and, because she was already two-and-twenty and had no man of her own, she had agreed.

So he'd wait for her after chapel and walk her home. They'd go to village dances together and one day he even hired a waggonette to take her down to Richmond for the day.

They didn't really think about marriage. To Betty it was all a bit of a lark and a chance to get away from the rather stifling atmosphere of home where, with two younger brothers and a younger sister, she had no privacy nor life of her own.

So when he started getting a little more intimate with her she made no great effort to resist.

Nonetheless, when she discovered she was pregnant it came as a profound shock. It was so unjust. It was only a bit of horseplay that had got out of hand. Other girls had got away with far more. But there was no getting away from the reality of her situation.

'Art certain?' he asked, the colour draining from his face.

'Sure as ah'll ever be,' she said.

'Hell and damnation!' he replied.

There was no way out of it. They would have to get wed and as soon as they could, before it showed. There were prying eyes and wagging tongues enough in any Dales village.

Her parents were livid. Her father, an irascible, ill-tempered man threatened to 'tan 'er hide' for letting it happen.

'But why did it 'ave to be Alfred Webster?' complained her mother. 'Couldn't thee've done a bit better than that, lass? The Webster's are common as mud.'

'At least,' thought Betty, 'it'll get me out of this house.' And it seemed that her frolic with Alfred might have been a good idea after all. Besides, he had a steady wage and they could surely find a cottage in the village to rent.

But just a week before the wedding came another bombshell. Alfred came round to her house, knocking on the kitchen door to avoid her parents.

'They're finishing me Friday,' he said, somewhat shamefaced.

'What?'

'Price o' lead's down i' London. Can't make it pay. Ending the shift. Mine'll 'ave to close soon,'

'What'll we do?' she asked.

The wedding went ahead as planned. There were a good number of people crowding into the chapel that September morning because the Thwaites were well known in both Wensleydale and in Swaledale, and Mr Thwaite was determined to do the thing in style, whatever the neighbours thought.

But straight after the marriage, Alfred Webster had to take his young wife to find work. He'd heard that the Midland Railway, building the new line from Settle to Carlisle, were seeking workers and pay was 'top rate'. If the money was good, they'd soon save up enough to get their own bit of land and start farming.

So they said goodbye to family and friends, packed up enough essentials for a few days and took the carrier's cart over to Hawes from where they were able to pick up another waggon to Ribblehead and Batty Moss.

What a sight greeted them as they came over the brow of the hill on the road from Hawes! There, in the hollow between the hills, a huge encampment stretched out. It was a shanty-town or, more strictly, a huddle of distinct shanty-villages, each with its own streets where men and their families lived whilst working on the great viaduct over Batty Moss, or the tunnel through Blea Moor.

Betty stared in amazement at the lines of men, like ants along the hillside, digging, driving machinery, carving masonry. Scaffolding was erected in several places through which a series of gigantic stone piers were slowly growing. Gangs were working together, hauling material. Cranes were lifting great squares of stone into position. There was movement everywhere. 'The building of the pyramids of Egypt must have been like this,' she thought.

When they arrived, Alfred was immediately directed to a foreman's office, and formalities were quickly completed. Yes, he would start on first shift tomorrow, with 'A' gang who were short-handed. Yes, there was accommodation for a married man. He was given a name and a number - Belgravia 17.

Each of the villages had a name redolent of the Crimea or the Wild West. There was Sebastapol, Inkermann, Salt Lake City, Jericho and, with consummate working-men's irony, alas lost on Betty, Belgravia.

But when Betty saw where they were to live, her heart sank. It was a simple hut of wooden frame and tarpaulin roof and walls, thrown up at speed and bolted together to provide basic shelter, nothing more. Heat and light was by oil stove and oil lamp, and they had to cook on the primitive stove. Everything smelt of paraffin. In the one room there were two simple beds with straw mattresses, a table, two chairs, a cupboard.

This wasn't what she had imagined for herself. She thought, a little tearfully now, of their small, low-roofed farmhouse. But at least this place was clean and she didn't have to share it with a younger sister.

They emptied their belongings on the table and soon filled the little cupboard. There was a jug and a bowl for washing. Where was the water?

'It'll not be fer long, lass.' said Alfred. 'We's'll save us brass and get a bit o' land. Just see if we don't.'

There was a knock at the door. They turned around. A woman, in her late twenties, introduced herself as Annie Beckett. Annie showed them where the facilities were - the latrines, which stank, the communal tap and even a little low cave where, in hot weather, families could keep perishables such as butter and cheese. 'You'll find these huts is 'ot in summer and freezin' i' winter,' she said, and Betty was to find these words only too true. When the sun blazed down for a few precious summer weeks between June and September it became too hot to stay in the hut and yet, in winter, the cold and damp seemed to penetrate every corner.

Betty found life difficult but, for a Swaledale farmer's daughter, no worse than the kind of thing she had been used to, though without the comforts of home. Alfred would work long hours each day except when the weather was too impossible, when they'd be laid off and he'd hang around the hut all day, or join the other lads in a game of rough football, or even a wrestling match.

Some days there'd be a fight. Each 'village' had its own champion or 'cock', usually a wild, bruising Irishman, and when challenged they'd fight, bare-fisted and stripped to breeches and stockings, until one of them lay senseless and bleeding. Heavy betting accompanied such bouts followed by heavy drinking.

Betty dreaded such occasions for, inevitably, Alfred would stagger home after midnight, paralytically drunk, sleeping on till well into the next day.

The Railway Company had organised makeshift facilities for its workers. There were shops - a baker's, a post office, the inevitable tavern, even a lending library as an attempt at something approaching intellectual improvement, and a school for the crowds of children, from new born babies-in-arms to the fully-fledged youngsters who raced in gangs around the villages creating nuisance. There were even regular visits by tradespeople from Ingleton or Hawes - bakers, greengrocers, a potter, a draper, a butcher, a milkseller - who plied their wares from the roadside.

Betty got to know several of the wives quite well, standing gossiping in the bread or meat queue. She enjoyed their company and soon knew the story of their lives. Many were Irish, having followed their men building both canals and railways for a score or more years. Some were from Devon, others from Scotland, and an increasing number were from the lead mines of the Dales which had hit hard times.

All agreed that this was one of the toughest and wildest railway contracts in Britain, only comparable to some of the Highland lines. Many had refused to stay but fled with their menfolk as soon as they could persuade them. But the money was good - a man could earn up to ten shillings a day - and jobs were not easy to come by.

'Money's good - if they don't sup it all up,' Betty's neighbour had said. Beer, she soon learned, was a major hazard. With nothing else to distract them, men spent hours at the tavern, consuming vast quantities of ale. Saturday night was worst. After being paid, many would drink themselves senseless and spend the quiet Sunday mornings, when no work was done, with deep hangovers.

The Railway Company even sent a preacher up from Bradford once a month, by train to Settle and then by waggonette, to try and install virtue in the large, migrant population. An excellent preacher he was too. He spoke of the evils of sin and of the demon drink, and the flames of hell-fire which awaited all sinners.

'And there's enough sinning goes on here, too,' Annie Beckett had informed her, not willing at this stage to elaborate, but Betty was soon to discover the women of easy virtue who hung around on Saturday nights to collect rich pickings from a willing clientele.

But when the preacher spoke the large congregation listened in respectful silence and joined in the uplifting hymns as if drunkenness and whoring were things that happened on another planet.

Another hazard was physical injury. Betty was told that of the two thousand or more workers, someone was injured almost every day. Scarcely a week went past without someone being killed. The hearse would be sent from nearby Chapel-le-Dale where the graveyard had already been filled and an overflow graveyard opened for railway workers.

Aware of its responsibilities, the Railway Company had actually opened a hospital and doctors were in regular attendance. She hoped they would care for her when her child came.

She was disturbed from her reverie by a blast of cold air as the door opened. He was standing there.

'Tha' idle bitch. Laikin' i' bed all t'day whilst ah've bin grindin' me fingers ter t' bone,' he snarled.

'Alfred, can't tha see ah'm badly,' she protested.

'Idle bitch,' he retorted.

She could tell by his manner, the slight slurring of his speech, that he'd already been drinking. It was only three in the afternoon. They must have laid them off early because of the weather and he'd been in the tavern.

'Tha's been drinkin',' she said.

'What if ah' 'ave? What's it to thee?'

'It's our brass. Brass we've to save....'

'Get this in thi' thick skull. It's my brass. I mek it. Theer. On't railway. Ah'll spend it 'ow ah pleases.'

He gazed down at her. She was aware that her pregnancy, now in a late stage, had puffed her face, making her look older, less attractive. Living in this dreadful place had worsened it. Her hair was in a mess.

'Get thee ter 'ell,' he said and stormed out, smashing the door behind him.

That's how it was, these days. What love there had been between them, if it was love, had soon disappeared, particularly as her pregnancy progressed and her slimness had disappeared under maternal plumpness. What had replaced it was a feeling of mutual hatred and contempt. He was drinking heavily and spending much of what he had earned, barely giving her enough to buy the food they needed, let alone putting aside the savings he had promised they would keep together.

And, worse, she suspected he was spending time with other women. Annie Beckett had hinted this strongly some time ago but wouldn't tell her more.

She lay in her bed for some time, gazing at the blank wall of the hut, her eyes filling with tears. So much for the promises he had made in chapel, and to her. Was this 'honouring' her?

She bit her lip with anger.

She'd have returned home, fled from him and this dreadful place but for the humiliation of having to present herself in front of her parents, admitting defeat, and of sharing a bedroom again with her thirteen year old sister.

She got up, lit the oil lamp.

There was little food in the house, but enough for her. He would be seeking sustenance in the form of ale.

She cut herself some bread, a little ham, cheese, and brewed tea.

Why should she put up with this kind of treatment, she wondered.

After all, was not Alfred Webster her inferior? This was 1871. Modern women didn't have to put up with this kind of behaviour.

She determined to shock him into changing his ways. Didn't she have rights, too? Wasn't he her husband? Why should he spend what should be hers in bouts of drinking?

She stood up. He would be in the tavern, right now. She would go down there and order him back, right now. If he didn't come, she would leave him, then and there. She wasn't going to be trampled on any longer.

She straightened her hair, pulled on her boots and fastened a thick shawl around herself. She had only been in the tavern once before, but she was well aware where it was. It was still pouring with rain outside as she threaded her way between the puddles towards the long, low hut which served as the camp tavern.

Inside it was crowded. A long bar ran the entire length of the hut on which there were a number of barrels from which the beer was being drawn. There were also bottles of whisky and gin behind the bar.

Drinkers sat at long rows of tables, rather like a canteen, replenishing their mugs as they were emptied. They gathered together in groups, some playing cards, others singing tunelessly.

She could see him in the far corner. He was with a crowd of about twenty, singing noisily. With him were two women. By their garish make-up she knew their trade.

As she walked across the smoke-filled hall, she knew that several pairs of eyes were on her and, pregnant as she was with her rain-soaked hair plastered down over her forehead, she was not looking her best.

But there was no retreat now. She had to press ahead with it.

She strode up to the group Alfred was in and pushed her way through, towards him. At first he didn't appear to notice her. She was trembling with nervousness. In this gathering, laughing, jesting and boisterous, he seemed so different to the sullen individual at home.

She stood there a few seconds, feeling conspicuous, dripping from the rain. Then he turned to her, seeing her there.

Suddenly the conversation died down.

'What does tha' want?' he asked her.

'Alfred. Tha's drunk enough. I want thee to cum 'ome', she said, her voice trailing away from nervousness, nothing like as strong or as certain as she had intended.

There was a roar of mimicking laughter from the group.

'She wants thee to cum 'ome,' said a raucous mocking voice.

'And get thi arse wiped,' said another. Titters of laughter. They were laughing at him as much as her, and he was humiliated. He hated it.

'Cum 'ome,' she repeated.

More gales of laughter.

'Or tha'll get thi lug 'oil clipped,' said the first mocking voice.

'I'll tell thi what ah'll do,' roared Alfred, leaping to his feet, grabbing his wife by the wrist. 'Any bugger as wants 'er can 'ave 'er, bairn an 'all.'

''Ow much is tha' sellin''er for?' said another voice. Guffaws of laughter, then silence as all eyes turned to Alfred. Suddenly everyone in the entire beer-hall seemed to be paying attention to what was going on. He was aware of the weight of eyes on him.

'Ah'll - ah'll tek a barrel of beer fer 'er!' he shouted.

'Ee's sellin' 'is wife fer a barrel of ale!'

Roars of delight. Betty turned scarlet, her eyes on the ground, too humiliated to move.

''Ool 'ave 'er fer a barrel o' beer?' shouted Alfred, now carried away with the idea, looking round the room.

Was he serious? Would he really? Or had the joke gone too far? The laughter began to die down.

Betty would have turned round and got out of the place but she was hemmed in at all sides. He was gripping her wrist.

'Who'll give me a barrel 'a beer?'

A long pause.

'I will,' said a voice. A roar of delight from the crowd.

'She's thine!'

A big, burly figure approached and seized Betty's hand. He was a toothless Irishman with a scarred face and enormous belly which flowed over his great belt and burst out of his shirt, a former prizefighter. A handful of money changed hands between him and Alfred and a barrel of beer was brought across from the bar and dumped on the table in front of them.

'Drink up!', shouted Alfred and the crowd pressed forward towards the barrel to enjoy free drink at the price of another man's wife.

Only the Irishman stayed back to admire his new aquisition, thrusting a great paw across her back and buttocks till she trembled with fear and humiliation.

She only knew she had to get out of this situation, come what may. She must keep a cool head. If she attempted to flee now, all would be up for her, and no doubt her baby too.

She could see that he, too, was drunk, almost as drunk as her husband, and by tomorrow would remember hardly anything of this whole disgusting episode.

So she sat quietly and awaited her opportunity. The Irishman was filling his glass from the barrel and soon would be lost in stupidity. But he came back to sit by her, pressing his clumsy attentions on her. She must bide her time.

Somebody was whispering in her ear.

It was a young man, he beckoned to her. She leaned to him. Her Irishman was deep in his cups.

'Listen, love, ah've seen what went on, an' it's shamefull,' he began. 'Ah'll create a diversion, an when ah do, you get out and 'oppit. Get away from 'ere. He's no use to you, that man o' yourn. They'll not come after thee, they're too drunk. Here - an' 'ave this ter 'elp thee ont' journey,' and with that he pressed something into her hand. Then, with a whoop, he leapt onto the table, kicking a pot of ale into the Irishman's face.

The whole room erupted. The Irishman leapt into the air and lunged at the young man, who sprang free and dashed through the tables. Betty saw her chance and flung herself at the door and outside the hut as the sound of smashing glass could be heard behind her.

She ran, but was soon out of breath, the weight of her child in front of her. She made her way as quickly as she could out of the camp, to the road. There was no one about.

Remembering where she was, she turned along the road towards Gearstones. Which way should she go? Would they follow her?

Instinctively she veered off to the left, along an old green way across the fields leading down to the river at Thorns Gill, where there was a deep little ravine crossed by an ancient packhorse bridge.

It was a beautiful place, a deep limestone gorge overhung by ash and rowan, with deep, brown pools where, on fine summer days, she had come with Alfred or by herself, to paddle and watch the trout laze through the water.

She remembered the way in the dark, alongside the wall, over the tiny bridge, then following the footpath along the now swollen stream up-river.

Could she find the way now? Going more by instinct than anything else she kept by the stream bank, feeling her way along and then, sure enough finding the crags and the nick in the crags, a shallow cave. She felt her way inside, out of the wind, relatively dry.

She crouched inside the cave, keeping what warmth she could to her. Only then was she aware of what she had been carrying in her tightly clenched fist - two hard, round objects, coins, which, from the shape and feel of them, she knew to be gold sovereigns.

From the bottom of her heart, she blessed her unknown benefactor.

It was too cold to sleep, but she got what comfort she could in the cave, instinctively keeping her body warmth within herself, wrapping the damp shawl around her, alternatively shivering and dozing until daybreak announced itself by a thin, grey light in the mouth of the cave.

She knew she must move from this place, seek shelter, safety. She was near her time. Where was the nearest place away from the camp? If she returned to the camp she would be reclaimed, whether by that dreadful ogre or her dissipated husband was no matter. Then she remembered her mother had a cousin in Dent - a Sedgewick. They would look after her, she was sure of that.

So she arose, cold as she still was, and walked back down the Gill, then along the path up to the road. It was still dawn and the camp was barely stirring. The old track she followed would go up above and behind the camp. With luck she might not be seen. Once she was safely on the fell, they wouldn't know she was there. She crossed the road and made her way along the old Craven Way, an ancient packhorse track from Settle to Dent which ran up behind the camp. The track began to climb and she looked across to the piers of the great viaduct now rising slowly. Beyond, Ingleborough mountain raised its massive bulk. In the cold, grey light of dawn it was an impressive sight. The mountainside was covered with a light scattering of snow. The temperature had dropped in the night, leaving a clearer, sharper day.

The way was now getting faint and she was climbing steadily. For a woman as close to her time as Betty it was an ordeal, even though she was a strong girl and used to walking the Swaledale fell paths. She walked slowly, breathing hard, aware of the extra weight in front of her, giving herself frequent pauses. The sun was rising from behind Cam Fell to the east, making the landscape shimmer with vivid beauty.

Perhaps they would see her up there and tell Alfred or her new possessor. She struggled on.

But by now the track had become no more than a faint sheep path and she could no longer be sure of the way. There was a junction - one way seemed

'She looked across to the piers of the great viaduct now rising slowly up. Beyond, Ingleborough mountain raised its massive bulk.'

to be climbing the shoulder of the fellside, towards Whernside's vast summit. She would keep ahead, towards an obvious pass between the hills, over Blea Moor itself, avoiding the great mounds of new clay and workings where deep tunnel-shafts were being built.

Soon she was at the top of the shallow pass and could look down towards the valley of Dent, like a narrow, green trough between the white-topped hills. She was now at the snow line and her footsteps crunched over the fresh new snow.

Suddenly the pain began, fierce, intense, so bad she had to sit down. It lasted for several seconds and left her white and shaking. She knew what it meant. Her baby was coming. She had no time to lose, she had to get into Dentdale, to seek help.

But it was still a long way and she could only move slowly, gripping her shawl around her shoulders. She must get there, come what may. Anywhere - the first farmhouse.

When the second spasm came it was even worse that the first. In spite of herself she had to sit down by a wall and cry out with pain.

Will Middleton, shepherd, was crossing Scale Gill Moss with his dog and a lamb rescued from a dead ewe. His alert ears heard the cry - a groaning. He paused, uncertain if his senses had deceived him. But no - there it was again, a groan like someone in agony, somewhere down below the top pasture.

He ran, with a dalesman's fast sure stride, down the fellside. Where had it come from? He paused again, ears straining. And then it came again - a women's cry.

He ran on, keen eyes searching for life. He found her hunched behind the wall. Had she been attacked or injured?

She was still writhing with pain, but it was subsiding.

'It's me baby,' she gasped. 'Comin''

What could he do? He had to get her down to the farm, but she was too heavy to carry.

'Wait,' he said, and he took off his jacket and wrapped it round her shoulders. Then he ran down the path to the farmhouse. Luckily his father was already outside. The older man was nearing sixty, but they struggled up the hillside to where the girl was lying.

They lifted her to her feet and, supporting her by each shoulder, her arms around their necks, half carried, half dragged her down the hillside to the little farmhouse.

'Put 'er int' spare room. I'll get some beddin' and a fire lit. Get Mrs Haygarth over,' commanded the farmer.

Will ran as if his life depended on it, vaulting gates. The Haygarths had the next farm.

'There's no time fer t' Doctor,' said Will, 'it's happenin' now.'

Dr Foster was down in Dent, some five miles away. Even by horseback, it would take an hour or two to get him to the top of the valley.

Mrs Haygarth, a middle-aged lady of not inconsiderable girth, panted behind Will and, when they got to the farm, Betty's pains were coming every few minutes. The birth was imminent.

'I'll need hot water. As much as you can get me. And towels, and some soap.'

The men hurried to fill kettles.

After a few minutes Mrs Haygarth was on the stairs.

'Will, wash thi' hands and roll thi' sleeves up. Ah'll need some help.'

'But it's not fella's work to be in there, Mrs Haygarth.'

'There's nowt that tha' 'asn't seen already or isn't goin' ter see sooner 'a later,' said Mrs Haygarth. 'Cum up quick.'

Will bounded up the stairs.

Mercifully, it was an easy birth. It was a girl and Betty, her ordeal over, relieved and thankful, held the little scrap of pink life close to her.

'Thank you, Mrs Haygarth. And thank you, Will. Tha' saved mi life,' said Betty, and she squeezed his hand.

'There were nowt to it,' said Will as he came downstairs to greet his anxious and astonished father. 'It were nobbut a lambin'.

When Dr Foster arrived, he congratulated mother and child and Mrs Haygarth for doing an excellent job.

'It's a bonny little daughter you have,' he said to Will.

'Nay - nay, it's not my bairn. Ah'm not wed,' protested Will.

'Oh - I see,' mused Dr Foster. Briefly they explained what had happened.

'Well, come what may, she must not be moved until she's completely strong. No wonder she's in such an exhausted state after what she's been through. Give her plenty of nourishing food - milk, eggs, soup.'

'That we shall,' promised Mr Middleton.

And the two men kept their pledge.

Before the day was out, Will appeared with a simply-made cradle under his arm, quickly knocked together from a bit of spare timber in the yard.

'It's a bit rough, but 'appen it'll do till we get little 'un summat better,' he said.

'But it's lovely,' she said.

She soon discovered why the two men were alone in the house. Mrs Middleton had died about eighteen months before, leaving father and son to look after themselves. No wonder the place had something of a run-down look.

She resolved as soon as she was well enough she would help set matters to right, to repay them for their kindness.

And it didn't take long for her to regain strength. Little Lucy Ann, as she was to be called, was born with her father's dark hair which soon yielded to feather-fine blonde down. The child fed and slept well and occcupied Will's cradle.

So Betty set to work with a will, cleaning, scrubbing, mending, cooking. She made clothes for the baby out of some of Mrs Middleton's old things, and adapted some for herself. Neighbours, such as Mrs Haygarth, called and left small presents of knitwear for the baby.

It was now spring, the sun warmer and, in the Dentdale hedgerows, the delicate flash of primrose indicated the rich promise to come. There was a gentleness in the air.

She cooked for the two men as they came back from the fells.

'Ah'm only earning me keep,' she said.

'Tha can stay as long as thi wants,' said old Middleton.

But one day there was another visitor at the farm. It was the Reverend Sumner, curate of nearby Cowgill Chapel. He'd heard about the new infant.

'Yes, vicar, we'd like to have her christened, as soon as we can. I'll be at church this Sunday and mebbe we can make arrangements then,' she said, anxiously. They were really Chapel folk, but surely it didn't really matter that much, did it?

'I'm sorry,' said Reverend Sumner. 'It isn't quite as simple as that. What about your husband, the child's father? He must be here, too. I gather it's only accident you're here at all,'

'Ah 'aven't got an 'usband,' she said.

'Why not?'

'Ee sold me fer a barrel o' beer?'

'What?!'

And so she explained the circumstances which had led to her night in the cave and her long walk across the fell.

'But it really won't do,' said the curate.

'Why not?'

'In the eyes of God Almighty, you and Alfred Webster are one flesh. Whatever he said to you in a drunken state in a tavern is of no importance. He is your husband until death do you part. You must go back to him and you must live with him as man and wife for the rest of your days.'

'But I don't want to. I've finished wi' 'im,' Betty protested. 'I'd rather die.'

'Don't talk like that. To talk like that is a sin. Think of your innocent child.'

'Ah'd rather stay here with Will and Mr Middleton. They need a woman here. Can't I be housekeeper?'

'It's utterly immoral. Living in this house, you a married woman and he an unmarried man.'

'Well, he's seen me givin' birth, an' ah can't think of 'owt else 'ees ter see of me.'

For once the loquacious Rev. Sumner was lost for words and could only flush scarlet. He would ignore that remark.

'You must write at once to the camp and your husband must come and fetch you,' he declared.

'But Batty Moss is no place to bring up a bairn.'

'That's not my problem, Mrs Webster. My concern is your spiritual welfare.'

There was no writing paper in the house, so the curate arrived next day with a pen, ink, envelope and stamp and under his instruction Betty had to write, in her neat, copperplate hand, to *Alfred Webster Esq, c/o Midland Railway Construction Camp, Batty Green, Ingleton, Yorkshire.* She was living with the Middleton's by Denthead and he was to come and bring her and their daughter back. She signed the letter reluctantly and the virtuous Reverend Sumner took it upon himself to ensure the letter was posted.

A week went by and nothing was heard from Batty Moss.

"Appen he doesn't want thi back lass,' said Mr Middleton over tea.

'Ah don't want 'im back, that's fer sure,' said Betty. 'Me an' Lucy Ann'll manage wi'out 'im.'

'Tha can stay wi' us,' said Will, 'as long as thi' wants. Isn't that right faather?'

'It is that, lad.'

But the Reverend Sumner was back after just over a week.

'We don't know if he received your letter,' he said.

'If he really wanted the lass, he'd find her,' growled Will. 'She's better off wi' folks as care about 'er.'

But the curate insisted that someone would have to go over to Batty Moss and find Webster and tell him.

'Can't leave well alone,' said Mr Middleton, shaking his head.

'God's will must be done,' responded Sumner frostily.

It was agreed that Betty could not go. The child had to be fed and it was too far to take her. Sumner would go himself.

So the following morning, he set out from Cowgill, over the moor to Denthead. He followed the great track now being built between the line of tunnels. He'd heard that contracts were being signed for the line in Dentdale and soon gangs of navvies - and their womenfolk - would be appearing to pierce the solitude of the valley.

'More trouble, more immorality,' he said to himself.

He was shocked to see the size of the encampment at Batty Moss. When he'd last passed along the road from Horton, there'd only been a dozen huts.

He looked for an indication of the Chief Engineer's office, or someone who could direct him, but before he did so a uniformed police officer stepped forward.

'Excuse me, Reverend, can I help you?'

'Yes officer. I'm trying to make enquiries about the whereabouts of one of the workmen here.'

'I'm sorry sir,' said the officer. 'Perhaps you haven't heard. There's been an outbreak of - of smallpox, sir. We're having to put part of the site in quarantine to ensure it doesn't spread, sir. And control all movement in and out of the site most carefully, sir.'

'Oh! - I see,' said Sumner, now extremely anxious. What kind of plague or visitation had come upon this place of iniquity?

The policeman directed him to a special office at the site. An official of the railway company was sitting behind the desk.

'You can understand our caution, Reverend,' he said. 'Smallpox is a very serious matter. We're getting every possible medical help to contain the outbreak, and the latest, specialist advice. The Company will spare no expense. But you understand when men - and their families - are living in such close conditions, disease can spread alarmingly quickly.'

'Obviously, we're trying to avoid any panic. There have been quite a few deaths already but we are certain that we've got the outbreak contained and there's only been four deaths so far this week.'

'But it does mean that there is some distress, you understand. Relatives come to find their loved ones and can't see them because they are in the quarantine hospital - we have an excellent surgeon, with wartime experience, in charge - we daren't allow them contact for fear of the disease getting out.'

'Worst of all, of course, is when you have to tell relatives that their dear ones have died.'

'Quite so,' said Reverend Sumner. 'But what I need to know is where one Alfred Webster, late of Gunnerside, Swaledale, is. He hasn't replied to a letter and we are a little anxious.'

'Did you say Webster sir?'

'Yes'

The officer shuffled papers on his desk. 'The name seems familiar. Wait a minute.'

He found the paper he was looking for. He paused.

'Did you say Alfred Webster of Gunnerside, near Reeth.'

'Yes.'

'I regret to have to tell you that Alfred Webster died yesterday afternoon of smallpox, in the field hospital. He is to be buried in Chapel-le-Dale next week.'

'How dreadful.'

'Was he married, sir? Did he have a wife? We've been unable to trace her on site.'

'Yes - he does - I mean did,' said the curate. 'And a new baby. Born about four weeks ago,'

'Did he know?'

'I don't know. Perhaps he received the letter we sent.'

'It's so tragic,' said the official. 'In years to come, people will never know the cost, in human terms, of building this railway.'

Reverend Sumner was given a bag containing Alfred Webster's poor possessions (his clothes were burned) and some women's things found in his hut. There was also a small wage-packet with an extra five sovereigns included by the Company.

'Not that the Company admits any liability,' said the official. 'It's what we call an Act of God. But where there's a wife involved, we like to be a little more generous than we have to be.'

'It's the Will of God,' said the curate.

When he returned with his news and the bag of possessions, he found Betty Webster curiously unmoved.

'I still can't find it within me heart to forgive what he did,' she said. 'But ah'm sorry he had to go in that way.'

They would never know if he knew about the birth of his daughter.

But what about Betty and her child?

Reverend Sumner was insistent about one thing. They could not stay at the farm.

Betty was perplexed. It was no use trying to go back to Swaledale, her parent's home was already overcrowded without a new baby. Indeed the curate knew of her cousin, one of very many Sedgewicks in the valley, but they, too, were a family of seven children and had no room for a cousin or her baby.

'I'm afraid it'll be the Union,' said the curate, hesitantly.

'You mean the Workhouse,' said Will Middleton.

'I can't think of any alternative,' said the curate.

'If 'er husband's dead and buried, doesn't that now mean she's free to wed again?' asked Will.

'Indeed it does,' said the curate.

Will Middleton turned to Betty.

'Ah'm not a fellah ter mek fine speeches or 'owt, Betty, but ah'm five and twenty and sound in wind and limb an' one day ah'll ave this farm, and if tha'd like to stay wi' us and wed me ah'll...'

The words dried up. He stood before her awkwardly, his hands twitching nervously.

'Don't you think this is all a little premature,' said the curate. 'Mrs Webster's had a great shock. She must have time.'

'Oh no vicar,' said Betty. 'You said so yourself. It's wrong fer me and my wee bairn ter live in this 'ouse with an unmarried fellah. What'll folk be thinkin' an' saying? Then we'd better make all the right arrangements, just as soon as we can. Right, Will?'

For answer, shy, as he was, Will Middleton leaned across and kissed her, in front of the curate, fully and passionately on the lips.

* * * * *

Rather more than eighty years later, sometime in the mid 1950s, a heavy steam-locomotive, hauling the 'Thames-Clyde' express, roared along the Settle-Carlisle line en route from St Pancras to Glasgow.

A frail, white-haired old lady in the dining-car leaned over to the gentleman sitting opposite her as they completed their lunch together.

'You know,' she said. 'My father helped to build the viaduct we're travelling over now.'

Her companion looked up from his meal across to the familiar view over Ingleborough.

'That's amazing,' he said.

'He died. Smallpox epidemic. Before I was born, I think it was. I used to go to a little church with my stepfather sometimes and he'd show me where they were all buried, those that died, my father amongst them.'

'Really?'

'Can't remember where it was exactly. Except a walk from Dent over the fell.'

Their conversation fell silent as the express roared and clattered into the tunnel, the big steam-locomotive panting hard.

As the train finally emerged from the other side, they looked down into the magical green valley of Dent.

'That's where I was brought up,' she said. 'Our farm was there, at the top of the valley.'

The train was now curving its way along the side of the fell, high above the dale.

'That's where I spent my girlhood,' she said. 'There, in that valley.'

Her companion looked down into a rich, green paradise of scattered farms and barns. In the distance the mountains rose up towards the sky.

'It's absolutely beautiful,' he said.

The train blasted its way through Dent's little mountain station without stopping. Then they were in the next tunnel and Dentdale was behind them. The locomotive shrieked and they were passing above Garsdale.

The old lady paid her bill and said goodbye to her companion, who stayed at the dining table awhile, smoking a cigar.

The train steamed into Appleby. A few passengers were alighting.

The dining car steward was clearing the table.

'Strange old biddy,' said the man, indicating where his companion had been sitting. 'Talked about her father building the railway and dying of smallpox.'

'She's often on this train, sir. Travels alone. Usually sits in the same seat. We try and keep it for her if we can, sir,' and the steward leaned over to brush the crumbs off the table. They'd soon be serving afternoon tea.

'I see,' and the traveller flicked ash into the neat silver ash-tray. From the platform there was a whistle and, with a judder and heavy panting from the engine, the train began to slip forward.

'There's no accounting for them, is there, sir?' continued the steward. The beat of the engine was accelerating.

'Who? What?' said the man, now losing interest in the conversation.

'Folk, sir.'

The traveller drew on his cigar and lay back in his armchair, his eyes slightly closed, the contentment of being warm and well-fed stealing over him and hurled at a mile a minute towards his Glasgow appointment.

The Scottish Pedlar

'Let's look at this old farmhouse!'

Jane's enthusiasm was infectious. The footpath actually ran behind the old farm but it was easy to leave the path and wander between the buildings at the front of the farm. Tony followed.

It was probably a mid-18th-century farmhouse with a solid, no-nonsense doorway leading into a little yard. The well-proportioned windows had lost their glass and the frames were sadly rotting away. It had been empty for some time. The massive stone slates, yellow with lichen, were missing from the roof, leaving rafters gaping. The house was in a sorry state.

Yet it was on the sheltered side of the valley, facing the sun and out of the cold wind which had turned a bright May morning into Antarctica. Celandines were out in the cracks between the paving stones and, along the hedge which led down the field into the little ravine, blackthorn was breaking into a delicate cream, sweet-smelling froth. It was a delightful place.

Her curiosity roused, Jane peered through one of the windows. The old cast-iron fireplace was still there and shreds of an floral wallpaper were hanging from the wall. Under the wallpaper was a pale green distemper. Elsewhere, the plaster was crumbling.

'Isn't it a shame,' she said. 'A place like this.'

Tony looked across at the old stairs, now rotting away to pulp where rain had poured in through roof and ceiling. It would only be a matter of time before the entire floor came away completely.

'It's beyond hope,' he said.

'But the walls are sound. It could be done up,' she said. 'People take over property in a far worse state than that and do it up.'

In that warm sunlight, away from the cold wind, it seemed the simplest thing in the world to suggest. Jane fantasised. 'Wouldn't it be super if we had the money and ...'

'Tha's trespassing!'

They turned round, startled. They hadn't seen the farmer who had come upon them unheralded. He had probably walked round the other side of the buildings.

He was a short, stocky man, in his sixties, wearing what appeared to be an old army coat fastened by a piece of string. On his head was a torn cap. His trousers, stuffed into a pair of wellington boots were striped and looked like part of an old suit.

'It was probably a mid-18th Century farmhouse with a solid, no-nonsense doorway leading into a little yard. The house was in a sorry state.'

'What yer doin' here? You can see the footpath doesn't go through 'ere.'

Tony and Jane were caught on the defensive.

'I'm sorry. We were on the footpath and ...' began Tony.

'... and we saw the farmhouse. And we thought nobody was around,' continued Jane.

'Well you thought wrong, didn't you,' said the farmer, pressing home his advantage.

'We're sorry. We only wanted to look,' said Jane.

'It's private property,' said the farmer.

Of course, but ...' began Tony.

'We only wanted to look,' interrupted Jane.
She was a pretty girl, with dark, appealing eyes. She saw her opportunity.

'We were wondering why it's empty,' she said. It's so nice here. We were wondering why nobody lives here.'

'They used to,' said the farmer 'A while back. But they left. It's a funny place is this. Nobody stays here long.'

'Why's that?' asked Jane.

The farmer hesitated, as if he didn't want to get involved. But then he visibly relaxed.

'It's a long tale. If tha' really want to know, go ask the missis. Tell 'er I sent thee.' And he gesticulated down the farm track, past his Landrover.

'Knock ont' door and ask 'er. Tell 'er I sent thee.'

'That's very kind of you. Thank you very much,' said Jane.

'Tell 'er I sent thee,' and he turned back to his work as if they no longer existed.

Tony looked at his watch. They really ought to have been on the fellpath by now. But it didn't really matter. They had plenty of time.

They soon reached the lower farmhouse. It was of a similar age and structure, but well cared for. A few late wallflowers, yellow and bronze, lined a strip of garden in front of the house. They knocked on the door.

The farmer's wife, a little, bird-like woman, slender and grey-haired, wearing a frock and knitted cardigan, appeared in the doorway.

'Yes?' she asked.

'Your husband - your husband said we might call and you would tell us about the old farmhouse. We were up there and asked him about it and he said to ask you.'

'High End? You want to know about High End?'

'Yes.'

'You're not writing a book or owt?'

'No - No,' said Jane nervously. 'We're just interested. We were passing. We just wanted to know about it.'

'You'd better come inside. Would yer like a cup of tea?'

'Thank you very much indeed,' said Tony. 'We'll take our boots off.'

'You needn't. It'll be alright.'

But their boots were encrusted with farmyard mud, so they left them at the door and padded across the stone floor of the kitchen in their thick socks.

It was a wide, low kitchen with dark beams with great hooks running across the ceiling. There was an Aga cooker, a fridge, a well scrubbed kitchen table and a couple of fireside chairs by a 1950s tiled fireplace.

'Just kick 'im off,' she said, indicating a black tomcat asleep on one of the fireside chairs, 'and sit theselves down.'

She took spoonfuls of tea from a small teacaddy and placed them in a large, brown teapot, adding scalding water from the kettle on the Aga. Soon there were two mugs of hot tea on the table and a plate of buttered scones.

'Thank you very much,' they said, appreciatively.

'You're a schoolteacher, aren't you?' she said to Tony.

'How do you ....?' began Tony.

'I can tell by your hands. You don't work with your hands.'

Self-consciously Tony looked at his slender, white hands, recalling the thick, muscular fingers and cracked nails of the farmer.

'Oh, don't worry, we get quite a few schoolteachers up here. We're quite used to them. Can be a nuisance when they bring kids with them. I used to be a teacher myself once.'

Jane looked up at her.

'Where did you teach?' she asked.

'Down in Pateley. Just infants. But I was born up here, in this very house. And when Tom said he'd marry me and bring me back up here, I couldn't say no, now could I?'

Tony took a scone. They were delicious.

'Are you two married then.'

'No - well, not exactly ...' Tony began, nervously.

'But we plan to be,' said Jane, looking across at him.

The farmer's wife smiled.

That's very nice.'

There was a short pause, as if nobody wanted to speak.

'So you want to hear about High End,' the farmer's wife began.

'Please,' said Jane.

'Now you mustn't take everything I tell you as being Gospel,' she said, almost without noticing it, slipping into teacher's English. 'When I was about your age and at College, we had - what do you call it nowadays - an assignment. Research. Finding out information for yourselves. I chose to do the history of this Dale. You know, I read all the old books. And spoke to lots of people. Especially old people. And one old lady, she must have been nearly 90, told me all about the old lead mines and the building of the reservoir and things she had heard about from older people when she was a girl. And that's how I heard about the Scottish pedlar.'

'As the story goes, in those days before cars or trains, people had to make most of the journeyings around by cart or on foot, so if you lived in the upper Dale, you didn't get around an awful lot. A trip to Pateley Bridge was like going to London nowadays and you might only go once a year to Pateley Races, as it was called in those days, with a big fair and a market.

'But there were quite a lot of pedlars or tinkers who would call at the farms, sometimes riding a horse or donkey, sometimes on foot carrying their wares in a little knapsack. They'd have regular rounds and would travel for miles and miles, sometimes sleeping rough or in wayside inns if trade was good. They'd come at the same time each year and if a farmer's wife needed a new kettle or needle, she'd wait till the pedlar called.'

'Now there used to be a Scotsman came this way each year - each Spring. He'd carry buttons, braid, ribbons, needles, brooches, pins, nice things, things you couldn't even get in Pateley Bridge.'

'And he'd travel in full Scottish costume - you know, Kilt, sporran, a plaid cloak, cap, always beautifully turned out. Part of his way of selling, I suppose. He'd bring his things down from Scotland to the Dales, and people would see him, recognise him.'

'From what people told me, he was a handsome, good-looking man, small and dark, like Lowland Scotsmen, you know, from Galloway or Ayrshire, usually are.'

'And from what people said, he was a bit of a ladies' man,' - and the farmer's wife looked at Jane. 'You know, had a nice way with him, would sit and chat to folk whilst he spread his wares out on the farmhouse floor.

'After all, in places like this, before cars, a body would hardly see a soul outside the farm from one year's end to the next, so a visit from a pedlar like him, with lots of news and gossip, was a real event. So he'd stay a while, perhaps having a bite to eat or sup.'

'And he even carried a little fife with him which he would play to announce his coming. Then he'd sit down just as you're sitting down and the farmer's wife would choose her ribbons and trinkets and they'd chat.'

'You know,' she said, 'he must have sat down in this very room many a time,' and she paused, as if to reflect on the handsome Scottish pedlar.

'Not,' she added, 'that there was ever any funny business. People weren't like that in those days. Or if they were, maybe they didn't talk about it. Though many a women must have been lonely, with her man out on the fells all day. A farmer's wife is too busy for any such caperings. But you never know what might have gone on ...'

'Anyhow, the pedlar came over from Scotland each year. He came down Wensleydale, then called at farms up Coverdale, before following the footpath over the fell-tops down into this valley. The path's still there.'

'That's the way we're going,' said Tony, 'We plan to take that path today.'

'Well let me know if you see any Scottish pedlars, won't you,' said the farmer's wife. 'You see, when he came into this Dale, High End is the first house he'd get to.'

'Now in those days a family called Blacker or Blackhaw - you see it spelt differently - lived there. They were a strange family. There'd been some quarrel in the past and the eldest son, Joshua, lived up there.'

'He was an odd man, unpleasant, bad tempered, nobody liked him. He was known to get drunk in the pub in Middlesmoor and to get involved in brawls. Nobody liked him.'

'Everyone felt sorry for his wife, Beth. She was a quiet, timid woman, and daren't say boo to a goose. He must have treated her something terrible. They didn't have any children. Perhaps it was as well.'

'Well, one day Blacker must have come home early and found the Scottish pedlar in the house, alone with his wife. Not that anything had been going on I don't suppose. They'd just be chatting.'

'But he was a jealous man. Never get yourself mixed up with a jealous man my dear,' she said, looking at Jane.

'No chance ....' said Jane, flushing, glancing at Tony.

'Jealousy's a terrible thing. It makes men totally unreasonable. And Blacker was a jealous man. Apparently he took up the pedlar by the throat, shook him and flung him out of the house, his pack and trappings after him, and told him if he ever found him on his land again he'd break his so and so neck.'

'What that poor woman had to put up with I can't imagine. That pedlar hadn't to call again and that was that. Luckily there were plenty of places for him to call at but everyone got to know about what had happened at High End, you can be quite sure of that.'

'Next year the pedlar didn't come into the Dale. At first every-one was quite surprised, for he hadn't missed a year for as long as most people could remember. People thought that perhaps he was ill, or he'd found a new trade.

'Then one day, about a month after he was due to come, they found him, or the remains of him. A shepherd stumbled across his body in a little gill, not far from the footpath. He was still wearing his kilt and his pack was there untouched but all his money had gone, every penny of it. His purse had been taken and there would have been quite a bit of money in it.'

'People had seen him as usual in Coverdale and he had left, as usual, early one day to cross the valley into Nidderdale but never arrived. He had been waylaid and murdered.'

'Now everyone remembered what Joshua Blacker had said to the pedlar. Everyone was convinced that Blacker had done it. He'd met him up on the fell and jealous man he was, killed him, then decided to rob him, hide the body and brazen it out. But there was no proof you see. There were no witnesses. Nobody could hang Blacker on rumour. It was really a dreadful state of affairs, Blacker openly defiant of local opinion and gossip. What his poor wife must have gone through I can't imagine.'

'Months went by and everyone assumed that he'd got away with it. Then, almost a year later, there was another visitor to High End.'

'It was a quiet Spring evening and Blacker was sitting down to Sunday tea with his wife. There was a heavy knock on the door three times....'

....and the farmer's wife demonstrated by rapping heavily three times on the farmhouse table.

'Beth Blacker opened the door and screamed. Standing there was a Scottish pedlar, dressed to the last detail as he had been in life, with his kilt, sporran, plaid cloak and knapsack and even his little fife by his side.'

'Mrs Blacker fainted quite away, and Blacker was staring, as white as a ghost himself. The spectre stepped inside the house and crossed to the table, as bold as brass, took off his knapscack and sat down as if he was going to join them for supper.'

'Blacker just stood there, as if struck dumb, unable to move from the spot. The ghost sat there a few moments, then rose up and without a word left the house, never to be seen again.'

'The effect on Blacker was extraordinary. From then on he was a shattered man. It was said that from that moment on he could never enjoy a quiet night's sleep but tossed and turned in frightful dreams. He refused his food, and visibly wasted away.'

'Within a year he was dead. And Beth simply abandoned the house, went away with her belongings, leaving the whole place as if its memories were too dreadful to contemplate.'

'Not long afterwards the truth was discovered. The Scottish pedlar had an identical twin, who, heartbroken at the news of his brother's death made enquires about how it had happened and was determined to revenge his death. So he disguised himself as his brother's ghost and sought vengeance on Blacker.'

'But the curious thing is this, the brother's curse seemed to fall across the house itself. No one seems able to live there. They try, but before long things go wrong and they leave. Nothing you can put your hand on, but no-one seems to be happy there. Things just go wrong. The last people - nearly 30 years ago - suffered just the same.'

She paused as if this recent history was too painful to probe.

'Will you have some more tea?'

'Thank you - thank you very much indeed, but no, I think we ought to be going,' said Tony.

They said goodbye to farmer's wife, thanked her warmly for her kindness, and laced on their boots.

'Do you think it's true?' asked Tony, as they walked back up the track towards High End. The farmer had gone. Though the sun still shone, no longer did the old farm look benign. There was evil in the gill.

'I don't think I'd like to buy it after all,' said Jane.

They re-joined the footpath. Soon they were climbing the fell. The valley began to open out before them. They could see High End, clearly, on the edge of the side valley and, just below, sheltered by trees, the farmhouse where they had met the farmer's wife. With the effort of their exertions the cold didn't seem to matter as much. All was space, light and the great panorama of the fells lay all around them.

On the brow of the hill, sheltering from the wind behind a drystone wall, they sat and ate their sandwiches. Tony took out the map, traced out the line of the route they would take to Coverdale that afternoon.

'Good God!'

'What is it?'

He pointed to the Ordnance Survey map, tracing the footpath as it climbed from the reservoir to the open fell. The name of the fellside:

'Dead Man's Hill.'